MITZI CLARK

&

THE SECRETS OF STASH

Grace Mirchandani

Copyright © Grace Mirchandani, 2022

Mitzi Clark & The Secrets of Stash
Copyright © 2022 by Grace Mirchandani
All rights reserved.

Without limiting the rights under copyright reserved above, no part of this publication may be reproduced, stored in or introduced into a retrieval system, or transmitted, in any form, or by any means (electronic, mechanical, photocopying, recording, or otherwise) without the prior written permission of the author of this book.

This is a work of fiction. Names, characters, places, brands, media, and incidents are either the product of the author's imagination or are used fictitiously. Any resemblance to actual events, locales, or persons, living or dead, is coincidental.

This eBook is licensed for your personal enjoyment only. This eBook may not be re-sold or given away to other people. If you would like to share this book with another person, please purchase an additional copy for each person you share it with. If you're reading this book and did not purchase it, or it was not purchased for your use only, you should return it and purchase your own copy. Thank you for respecting the author's work.

First Edition, 2022
Published in the United States

Editing: Genevieve A. Scholl
Cover Design: Sinisa Poznanovic

DEDICATION

This book is for the kids (of all ages) who have
supported my writing journey so far.
You keep me writing. *You* keep Mitzi Clark alive and
I *love* telling her stories.
From the bottom of my heart, I appreciate you all.

CHAPTER ONE

Someone would end up dead. She just knew it. She couldn't shake off her feelings of guilt, knowing that, here she was off to training camp in Alaska for the summer, while everyone she loved was back home, fighting a secret war against unnatural creatures. One way or another, Mitzi Clark knew that this was gonna be a summer to remember.

Mitzi rubbed her face, already tired from the long flight. They had been in the air for four hours, and there was still so far to go. Thankfully, her best friend and travel companion, Rose, let her have the window seat. Rose had been on a plane before and told Mitzi that everyone should have the window seat on their first flight. Rose was out cold the majority of the flight, only waking up for a few minutes when the flight attendant came by with lunch.

Mitzi pressed her forehead against the cold, little window and tried to take a nap, but the craziness of the past year kept her mind running at a restless pace.

She thought back on her life before she knew the truth about her parents. Everything was so much simpler back then, so carefree. Even though it had only been a year, it seemed like a whole lifetime ago. It's funny how quickly life changes the instant you find out your parents hunt monsters for a living. Not only because everything you believed about your parents was wrong, but also because you find out about the true existence of monsters in the first place.

Her breath fogged the glass of the window and she closed her eyes, wondering what life would be like now if they had never found the clues that led them to uncover the truth. She would still believe her mother was just another ordinary mother, and her father, just a regular old lawyer.

But as it turned out, her parents were *far* from ordinary. As far as possible. Her parents, Ben and Deb Clark, were members of The Society for Hiding Undesirable Truths, or SHUT. Her father was actually the leader of the whole northeastern United States! But the real kicker was that SHUT's headquarters was underneath her house the whole time, in an underground chamber called The Den, and she never even knew it was there.

She would never have found out the truth about her parents without her two best friends, Rose and Finn. Mitzi cracked open her eyes and glanced at her sleeping pal, and felt a surge of gratitude rush through her. She couldn't imagine being on her way to training camp without Rose. She shifted her weight in her chair, and her thoughts drifted to Finn, off on some other plane with his parents, to a made-up cover-story camp. *Crazy, the lengths SHUT goes to, to keep people from knowing about the existence of non-human creatures.* Most of the kids on their way to camp were the children of other SHUT members. But a handful of kids were recruited from families that had no knowledge of SHUT, and the cover-story camps were created to keep it that way.

Finn's parents thought he would be spending the next six weeks at an all-boys dude ranch, where he would learn the ways of the old cowboys and become a "real man." The reality was, as soon as they left him there, he would be put on a plane to Camp STASH, his real destination. There were several camps set up like that. Filled with fake counsellors, fake cabins and lunch halls, fake *everything*. It was remarkable, the lengths SHUT went to, to keep the organization a secret. The whole thing was quite amazing, really.

"Wonder what Finny is doing right now," Rose grumbled, startling Mitzi.

Mitzi sat up straight in her seat and looked at Rose, whose eyes were still closed. "That's funny," she said. "I was just thinking about him checking into his cover camp with his parents."

Rose's eyes opened in a flash and she sat up abruptly. "Shhh," she snapped. "Careful, Mitz. You never know who is listening."

A fire rolled into Mitzi's cheeks. "Dang. You're right. Sorry."

"I bet he is pretty miserable." Rose laughed, and put her head on Mitzi's shoulder. "His dad was so proud when he heard Finn wanted to go and 'learn how to be a real man!' at the dude ranch."

"I know!" Mitzi chuckled. "His father really hates that he spends so much time with the two of us girls. Can you imagine what would happen if he knew that…"

"If he knew," Rose interrupted, "that Finny was really camping with us girls all summer, he would *never* let us hang together, ever again, I imagine."

The pair fell silent for a few moments.

Rose reached her hands above her head and stretched out as best as she could in her small airplane seat. "How much longer do we got?" she asked. "My back is stiff and my butt feels like a giant pancake."

"Couple hours." Mitzi sighed. "Then just one more flight to camp from there."

Rose looked at Mitzi and her face became suddenly serious. "Are you nervous about camp at all? You seem so chill about the whole thing."

"Are you kidding me?" Mitzi raised her eyebrows. "I'm a wreck. But it's not so much about camp. It's all the other stuff."

"What other stuff?" Rose asked.

"You know," she lowered her voice to a whisper, "the stuff going on back home. I feel like we should be there to help."

"Oh. That," Rose said, nonplussed. "It's been quiet for months. I'm sure that they can handle whatever happens without us. Is that all you are worried about?"

A mischievous look spread across Rose's face. She pointed over her shoulder toward the back of the plane. "You're sure your nerves have *nothing* to do with the fact that your future boyfriend Trent is on his way to camp with us, too?"

"Rose! SHUT UP!" Mitzi said as she playfully grabbed Rose's hand down and elbowed her in the ribs. "I don't want to talk about it! Besides, he hasn't even so much as made eye contact with me. Please, don't make it weird."

"Oh, girl," Rose laughed, "I will let it be for now. But don't think for a second that I'll let the summer go by without making sure you two get together."

"Fine! Fine. Just drop it for now!" Mitzi said as she turned and rested her forehead on the window again. "I think I'm going to just take a nap until we get there."

With her head again pressed against the cool window pane, a million thoughts swirled inside her head. Thoughts of Finn walking around a fake camp with his parents... of what camp might be like... of secret wars and dark creatures. Of *him*. Her thoughts flashed through her mind's eye like her brain was scrolling through vlog reel after reel, and before she knew it, she slipped off into a deep sleep.

***

What felt like only minutes later, a metallic

crackling man's voice filled the airplane, stirring Mitzi awake. It was the pilot announcing their descent. Next to her, Rose clipped her tray table back into the seat in front of her, put her chair back to the upright position, and tightened her seatbelt. Mitzi, unsure of what she needed to do, tightened her belt as well. It felt strange to be descending. The plane made a grumbling noise and Mitzi's eyes widened, not knowing what it could mean.

"Relax, girl," Rose said calmly, taking Mitzi's hand. "That sound is just the landing gear. It scared me the first time, too."

"Oh. I guess it did freak me out a little bit," Mitzi admitted, loosening her grip on Rose's hand. "Was it that obvious?"

"Your eyes got huge!" Rose teased. "You were like this." Rose stretched her eyes open as far as she could and contorted her face, pulling her chin all the way back, until most of her teeth were exposed in a hilarious snarl.

"Oh my God! No I was not!" Mitzi cracked up at her dramatic friend.

"Girl, I know," she said. "But I made you laugh and forget about the fact that we are coming into land now, didn't I?"

"Yes, you did." Mitzi smiled as the plane screeched a tiny screech as its tires landed smoothly on the runway.

"The plane continued to slow down and Rose turned again to Mitzi, letting go of her hand. "See? Nothing to it."

"Right. Now to find our *next* plane." Mitzi sighed.

"You know, something just occurred to me," Rose said. "I bet our next plane will only have campers on it."

"Oh yeah, probably," Mitzi agreed.

"It may even be," Rose paused for dramatic emphasis, "just *three* of us."

"Crap." Mitzi deflated. "Here we go."

Chapter Two

It wasn't only the three of them on the next plane. It was six. Rose was right to assume it was all campers, though. Mitzi, Rose, and the still-not-making-eye-contact Trent were joined on their next small plane by three very annoying girls, who seemed to be sisters. As the girls scrambled into their seats, they were bickering with each other and didn't notice, or at least they didn't seem to care, that they were in the company of others. Two of the girls looked like they may have been twins, but Mitzi didn't feel comfortable looking at them long enough to confirm.

They all looked perfect. One of the twins had chin length blonde hair and was dressed in athletic and sporty looking clothes while the other was wearing all pink and had her golden hair in neat French braids, tied with bows. The third sister looked to be a couple years older and taller than them. She had long flowing blonde hair that almost seemed to sparkle with her every movement.

It was a small plane, but much larger than the six of them needed. On one side were two seats, and across the aisle was a single seat. It was some kind of private jet, probably owned by SHUT. Mitzi and Rose took the two seats together in the very last row and Mitzi hoped that Trent would sit somewhere nearby but was disappointed when he chose the single seat in the very front row.

Why does it seem like he's avoiding me? Ugh! Oh well, Mitzi. Get a grip.

The older of the three girls took a single seat a couple of rows behind Trent and the other two sat together a few rows in front of Mitzi and Rose. It was so quiet on the plane. Even Rose was quiet, which Mitzi found odd because usually Rose was the one to introduce herself first around new people. Mitzi loved her outgoing nature because it took the pressure off her to be social. Besides, what if they weren't campers, too, and were just on the same plane? The only thing Mitzi knew for sure was that this was the last plane on the way to camp. Maybe someone would meet them when they landed and take them on to camp from there, like on a boat or something.

But after a couple more minutes of silence, the pilot came in and stood in the aisle, next to where Trent was sitting.

"Hey, Campers!" he said.

Mitzi felt her shoulders relax a bit with the confirmation that at the very least, she was amongst other SHUT campers.

"I am Captain Frank, here to welcome you all aboard Turbo Grand Air, one of SHUT's many private jets." He cleared his throat and smiled, looking at each person, one at a time. "You lucky six are off to Camp STASH, where you will learn the skills needed to become fully-fledged, contributing members of the SHUT organization. We will be taking off within the next twenty minutes or so and will be landing on the island in a couple hours. We don't have a flight attendant on this flight but I'll announce when you can get up to use the restroom. Otherwise, stay seated and belted in and enjoy the ride."

He turned with a small wave and went into the cockpit, but the silence remained for several moments before Rose blurted out, "I was hoping there would be food! Is anyone else starving?"

"Heck yes!" one of the younger girls answered.

"Haven't eaten a thing for hours. I'm starving."

"Oh relax, Mimi," the older girl snapped. "There is a big welcome picnic when we get there. You know that."

"I wasn't talking to you, Bella," she said. "I was talking to the girl back there. Girl, what's your name?"

Rose shot Mitzi an annoyed look before answering. "I'm Rose, and this is my best friend, Mitzi."

Bella turned and craned her neck to get a good look at them. "Mitzi? As in Mitzi Clark?"

Mitzi was dumbfounded. How did this girl know her name? Why did this girl know her name?

"Um, yeah," Mitzi managed. "How do you know who I am?"

A giant grin spread across Bella's face. "Girl, are you serious right now? Everyone knows who you are. Not too many kids come to camp already full working members of SHUT. You're, like, famous."

"Oh God." Mitzi squirmed in her seat. She didn't want to be famous. She just wanted to go to camp and be another camper, like everyone else. "It's no big deal what we did, you know. Me and Rose and our friend Finn, too."

"No big deal?" Bella was practically yelling. "Correct me if I am wrong here, but you three discovered SHUT's northeast secret Den, saved a bunch of people from a mimic attack, and recovered one of the Dark Trinity blood vials! I would call that a big deal."

"I was just in the right place at the right time." Mitzi looked at Rose, hoping she would interject and change the subject. "Anyone would have done the same thing."

"Well, whatever you say," Bella flicked her hair

over her shoulder, "you are definitely gonna be miss popular at camp this year."

"Ugh." Mitzi groaned and pressed her head back into her seat, closing her eyes. "Great."

"Oh, don't worry about it, Mitzi," Rose said. "Maybe she's exaggerating. I doubt *everyone* at camp has heard about us. Maybe her family knows your parents and…"

"It's okay, Rose," Mitzi grumbled without opening her eyes. "Once everyone figures out how boring and normal I am, I'm sure they will back off."

"Don't worry, girl," Rose said just above a whisper. "I'll do my best to draw all the attention to me. You know I love the drama."

Mitzi opened her eyes and looked at her best friend. "Thank God for that."

The flight went by uneventfully after that. In fact, no one said a word at all, which Mitzi thought was a bit strange but enjoyed the quiet, not knowing what it would be like at camp when they arrived.

The pilot's voice crackled through the speaker, breaking the silence to announce their approach. Mitzi's body stiffened, suddenly nervous about their arrival.

"Hey," Rose elbowed Mitzi in the ribs, "are you sure you are cool?"

"I guess maybe I am feeling a bit nervous about camp after all," Mitzi admitted.

"Well, just try to relax because I have a feeling that we are about to have the most epic summer of our lives."

Chapter Three

Mitzi watched out the window as the plane circled a small island. She could see a few buildings and a lot of trees, but not much else. The landing was a bit bumpier than she expected but she was happy to finally be on the ground. She took a few deep breaths, in an effort to calm the nerves that were still very much dancing around inside of her. Trent was the first to walk out, followed by the trio of blonde sisters, leaving Rose and Mitzi as the last to disembark.

Mitzi felt confused as she walked down the steps from the plane. Looking around, she expected to see a bunch of people, or at least a few. Instead, they arrived to no one, and a big, empty field with a tree line in the not-too-far distance.

As she took her last step down onto solid ground, Mitzi was startled by the pilot's voice behind her. "Strange, right? I remember my first time here, too. I wondered where the heck everyone was!" He laughed, as the rest of the group turned to look at him, their faces looking equally befuddled.

He stopped laughing and his face transitioned into a more serious expression. "Welcome to the Camp STASH Airstrip. A senior camper," he pointed at Bella, "will be bringing you in to registration. Until exit day at camp, you are not to return to the airstrip. It is unsafe and out of bounds. Do you understand?" He took turns looking at each of the campers before him, each acknowledging with a quick nod or a "yes."

"This is where I leave you then. See you in six weeks and please enjoy your summer." He turned on the spot and disappeared back up the stairs and onto the plane.

"Alright, listen up!" Bella commanded much louder than necessary. "See that opening there in the tree line? We take the path there, through the woods to camp headquarters. It's about a thirty-minute hike so let's get to it. I'm tired and I want to get there quickly, so no fartin' around. Especially you two. I mean it, Mimi and Jayde. Don't piss me off." She glared at her sisters, and Mimi stuck her tongue out in protest.

"Piss off," the other sister said. "You're not the boss."

"Whatever, Jayde," Bella snapped. "Just move it."

The six campers trekked through the field quietly, and soon came to the mouth of the forest path.

"Looks creepier than I thought it would," Rose whispered to Mitzi, who was shifting her duffle bag from one shoulder to the other. "And you know how much I just love bugs."

"At least it's still light outside. I feel like it should be so much darker than it is. Makes sense with the time change, though." Mitzi shrugged at Rose, and the group all shifted to walking single file down the narrow dark path.

"Shoot." Rose giggled. "You know, I forgot all about the time change. No wonder I'm so dang tired. It's like 9pm at home and we haven't even had dinner yet."

"That makes it, like, 6 here, right?" Mitzi asked loudly so that anyone would answer.

"Close." Trent's voice was a bit hard to hear from the front of the line. "It's actually 5."

"Which we all would know if they let us have our phones, ugh," Bella whined. "It's really the only thing I hate about being here. Stupid 'no phones allowed' rule. I mean, some of us have *lives* back home, you know. Stupid."

"It does suck," Rose agreed. "But I get it. I'm sure it's a security thing."

They walked and walked, Mitzi's feet growing more tired by the minute. The rhythmic crunching of branches under their feet and the occasional chitter of a chipmunk, or call of a bird, the only sounds as they made their way along the path.

A sudden light tapping sound, brought Mitzi's attention above her. It was starting to sprinkle. The leaves on the trees alerting the group to the arrival of rain, before they could feel it. It went from a couple of soft drops of water falling, to a full out torrential downpour within a matter of seconds, sending the group sprinting down the now-muddy forest trail.

"Bugs and rain!" Rose shouted above the rush of the water. "My two favorite things."

Mitzi laughed at her friend, now running with her large duffel bag held high on top of her head in a ridiculous effort to keep dry.

"You do know you're in South-east Alaska, right?" Mimi yelled back at Rose as she continued to run. "This place is pretty much known for bugs and rain."

"I know, I know," Rose whined. "Doesn't mean I gotta like it."

Bella stopped running to catch her breath, sending her sisters crashing into her. "You can't just stop running, Bella!" Jayde shouted angrily as she fought to find her balance. Trent, who was in the front, heard the tussle and stopped as Bella announced, "It's just around the bend, you guys. Just go in and find the new camper registration table. You can't miss it."

A shiver ran through Mitzi's body as she

turned the bend and the back of a giant log cabin stood towering before her. She was cold, covered in mud, and soaked to the bone. She wasn't going to make the first impression she was hoping to make.

Bella took off around the right side of the building, leaving the five new campers on their own, without a single bit of further guidance.

Mitzi watched as Trent took off behind Bella. With a shrug of her cold and soaked shoulders, Mitzi followed suit with Rose, Mimi, and Jayde squishing their way behind her. As she rounded the front corner, for the first time, Mitzi got a look at Camp STASH. She could see several groups of cabins, scattered around a giant field. At the far end of the field she could make out another large building, like this one, and an outdoor pavilion. There wasn't another camper in sight. The rain was dumping so hard that it was impossible to hear anything else, but

Mitzi assumed all the other campers were already inside creating a buzz louder than the hallway on the first day of school.

The five ran up the front steps and onto a giant covered porch, taking a moment to gather themselves and shake out a bit of the rain they had collected, before entering the giant crowded reception hall. Rose cocked her head to the side and squeezed her long braids, a stream of water flowing onto the floor. Trent kneeled over his bag, routed through it, and took out a hoodie, which he pulled on right over his soaked clothes. Jayde and Mimi stomped their feet, unsuccessfully trying to knock away the extra water. Mitzi just stood there watching them and shivered, knowing there wasn't much she could do until she could get into warm and dry clothes.

"Nothing to it but to do it!" Mimi said as she

opened the big red front door and walked in followed by her sister and then Trent.

"You ready for this?" Rose smiled a big smile at Mitzi.

"Yeah. I just want a moment to catch my breath first," Mitzi mumbled. She didn't think she would ever really feel ready, but after a minute, she let out a long sigh and said, "Let's do this."

As the door swung open before her, Mitzi's ears were blasted with a roar of jumbled voices that were now too close to be drowned out by the still heavy rains. In front of her, a sea of colors and faces blended and moved, making her feel a bit comforted, thinking she could slip in without being noticed at all. The room was very large, with a pitched ceiling. Mitzi's nose burned slightly, hit with a blast of air that was a cross between a fart and a wet gym sock, probably from too many stinky and rain-soaked teenaged boys crammed into the space. There were colorful banners hanging all around the room that said things like, **Health Check** and **Supplies**. Just as a crushing sense of overwhelm started to creep over her, Mitzi's eyes settled on a banner that relaxed her instantly: **New Campers-Start Here.**

Mitzi pointed at the banner and yelled to Rose, "I don't think they could make it any easier than that."

Rose's eyes were wide with her own nervous energy. "Thank God for that."

Chapter Four

The pair made their way through the crowds, occasionally bumping into other campers, busy mingling with their own friends, and Mitzi was pleased to see there was not a line at the New Campers table. There was, however, a short, plump, cheery-faced woman with short gray curly hair, smiling at them from her seat behind the table. She was clutching a tablet against her chest and her whole body seemed to vibrate, like she was bubbling with the excitement of seeing them walk up to the table.

"Well, hello, ladies, and welcome to camp," she practically sang. "I know who you two are and I gotta say, although maybe I shouldn't say, I am a big fan of both of you."

Mitzi froze. She couldn't believe this lady

knew who she was. How did she know? It wasn't like they had on name tags or anything. Rose must have been thinking the same thing because she blurted, "How on earth do you know who we are? We *just* got here."

"Oh dear me," the lady's face flushed bright red. "I didn't mean to freak you out. My name is Linda and I am the Camp STASH Head Counselor. I am also the one who coordinates the flights and boat arrivals. I pretty much know who to expect and when. I have already checked in the other campers that were on your flight, so *that's* how I knew who you are!"

"That makes sense," Mitzi mumbled before trying to change the subject with, "So, what do we need to do?"

"Oh! Right!" She chuckled, and, with her free hand, started sorting through papers in a small box on the table before handing each girl a small white card. "Here are your schedules, along with your work and cabin assignments. What you need to do now is make your way around the room, stopping at each table. Once you're done, just hang out for a bit. Your flight was the last to arrive, other than our cover flight, which will get in very late tonight. You'll be released for free-time here shortly, to get settled into your cabins. Then we will all meet up for the welcome picnic dinner in the pavilion at seven."

The girls nodded at Linda as they moved away toward the next table. Unfortunately, Linda decided to yell her goodbyes as they left.

"So happy you are here with us, Mitzi Clark!"

Her voice rang throughout the entire room and in a split second, the noisy cacophony of the room became as silent as a funeral, all eyes turning toward Mitzi and Rose. Mitzi wanted to run out of there with her face covered, but instead kept her gaze focused on the table ahead. Her cheeks were on fire and she could feel a thousand eyes on her.

"Alright, you all!" Rose yelled and waved at the crowd, a huge smile plastered on her face. "Carry on, carry on, nothing to see here. Go about your business."

The room started to buzz slowly again, and a tired and irritated Mitzi glanced back at Linda, who mouthed the word "sorry" to her. Mitzi didn't think that she seemed very sorry, though. It was almost like Linda did that on purpose. But why? *Oh well*, thought Mitzi. *At least that's over with.*

"You okay?" Rose whispered. "That was messed up."

"I'm fine," Mitzi said as she looked down at her card. "Just please tell me that we are in the same cabin. I'm in cabin four."

"Well, I could tell you that I'm in cabin four, too, but I'd be lying. I'm in Cabin One," Rose said as they approached the table.

Mitzi was annoyed. "Son of a…"

"Hello, ladies!" a very handsome man, who looked to be in his early twenties, interrupted her from behind the table. "I am Nurse Alex, and you don't need to introduce yourselves because Linda just did it for you. She's a total hoot."

"Hoot isn't the word I was thinking, but okay. So, *you're* the camp nurse?" Rose asked, sounding a bit too impressed.

"That I am," he said. "I also give out the work assignments around here so you better be nice to me. As it is, I hooked the two of you up, and your boy Finn, too, but don't tell anyone."

Mitzi's forehead crunched, unsure of what he was talking about. "What did you hook us up with? I don't get it."

"If you look at your card, you will see under 'jobs' it says Health from three to five. That means you are stuck with me from three to five, five days a week, and it's the most boring job at camp. I had to call in a few favors, but I really just wanted to hang with the three of you. Selfishly, I'm dying to hear your stories of what really went down and how you managed to infiltrate SHUT."

Mitzi was embarrassed. "It's not really very interesting, so you know…

"Of course it is," Rose said, batting her eyelashes at Nurse Alex. "We can't wait to tell you all about our adventures."

"Great!" Alex said. "I didn't think you would mind. Beats dish duty, cleaning, or cooking. Everyone gets a job, for ten hours per week, might as well have the best one."

He winked at Mitzi, and she could feel her cheeks burning again. She glanced over at Rose, who seemed to be in some sort of trance. Gross. He was handsome, sure. But something seemed strange about this grown man wanting to spend his time with three teenagers.

Or maybe it wasn't strange at all. Mitzi was tired and her exhaustion was making her feel paranoid.

"Thanks for hooking us up with a chill job," she managed. "We still have quite a few tables to get to. Do we need anything else from you, for now?"

He stood up straight and scrolled through his own tablet. "No medications, no allergies for either of you, so you are all set."

"Wait til you talk to Finn." Rose giggled.

Mitzi and Nurse Alex laughed, releasing whatever tension Mitzi was still feeling.

"I know, I know," Nurse Alex said. "I saw his chart already."

"He sneezes more than any human I have ever met," Mitzi added.

"Can't wait to meet him," Nurse Alex said. "You better get a move on it, girls; looks like Mr. Bell is waiting for you."

The girls turned to the next table to see a middle aged, balding, red-faced man staring at them.

"Don't worry," Nurse Alex added. "He's not as bad as he looks."

Mitzi looked over at Rose. "I hope not."

Mr. Bell's red-faced stare disappeared into a warm smile as the girls reached his table. He was sweating a little more than seemed normal to Mitzi, but she thought maybe he just wasn't feeling well. Plus, it was a little warm in this corner of the big room.

"Hello there, young ladies," he said. "My name is Mr. Bell and I'm the Tech instructor around here, but today my job is to hand out your supplies." He grunted as he reached under his table and produced two identical black backpacks, stuffed to the max, and set them onto the table with a thump. "Got all the stuff you'll need for classes and two sets of training clothes."

"Training clothes?" Rose whined.

Mr. Bell rolled his eyes and replied in what sounded like a scripted answer, "Training clothes are to be worn during weapons training class at all times. You may wear your clothes from home the rest of the time you are here at STASH."

"I guess I can deal with that," Rose grumbled.

"Now you two girls better get a move on it," he said as he pushed the bags toward them. "You still have a few tables to hit and it's almost time to clear out to the cabins."

"Thank you," Mitzi said as she and Rose snatched up the bags and moved to the next table, the room growing louder by the minute.

The last three stops were brief. They received a tablet and some sort of smart watch at the first, had to fill out a couple forms at the next, and at the last, a really old cheerful lady named Verna gave a rundown of the Snack Shack, the camp store. Verna told them how to earn extra camper coins, to spend on stuff like calls home, snacks, and toiletries. The jobs that they'd have on campus put regular coins in their shack account to spend in there, and no real money was ever exchanged. Mitzi thought the concept was pretty cool.

"So that's the purpose of jobs!" she said.

Verna smiled at her sweetly. "That, and to keep all of you kiddos out of trouble. Too much free time can be a dangerous thing, when a bunch of teenagers are concerned."

"Works for me," Rose said. "You know how much I love to shop! I was wondering how I would get through the whole summer without…"

A loud bell rang throughout the big room, interrupting Rose and quieting the space instantly, followed by a loud and bubbly announcement blaring through the speakers.

"Welcome, Campers! I am Deana D., and I'll be your Stations Master this year. I'm in charge of the music 'round here so if you have any special requests, come by the tower or message me and I'll see what I can do. But, for now, it's time to check out those cabins, get settled, and keep an eye on your wrist! Your new watch will buzz when it's time for the picnic! Now, off you go!"

The doors flung open with a bang and the

crowd pushed their way out in a less-than-orderly rush, as Mitzi stood watching, waiting for it to clear out a bit before trying to leave.

"I really wish we were in the same cabin," Rose said over the departing crowd.

"I know," Mitzi agreed. "I'm feeling a bit nervous with the thought of not being together, but I guess we will survive."

"Come on," Rose blurted, and hooked her arm through Mitzi's, leading her out of the hall. "I will walk you to your cabin first and then head off to mine."

"Rose, you really are the best." Mitzi smiled and squeezed her arm. "Plus look! It's stopped raining!"

A deep voice from behind them on the porch startled them. "Don't get used to it," a tall and skinny, older boy with dark hair said. "It rains all the time here. But I don't suppose it will bother the great Mitzi Clark, will it?" He pushed past the girls, knocking into Mitzi, despite there being plenty of room to walk around them, and stormed off angrily, out into the field.

"What in the hell was that all about?" Rose yelled loud enough for him to hear.

"I have no idea," Mitzi said, a bit shaken. "But I think it's safe to say, at least one person here at camp doesn't like me very much." Mitzi shrugged her shoulders, bewildered at the whole thing.

"Then we know at least one person at camp who is a *dumbass*," Rose said. "Let's go. Let's not let that fool ruin our fun."

And they were off.

Chapter Five

The cabin was filled with new faces and loud chattering, both of which made Mitzi feel a little unnerved. She scanned around the room and took everything in. It looked a lot like the cabin at her old summer camp. There was just a bunch of metal bunkbeds lined against both walls, each with a wardrobe between them and a large trunk on the floor at the end. She glanced around at the faces of the other girls, hoping to see someone familiar, like one of the twins from the plane, but quickly realized she was alone.

"Hey," a voice snapped her out of her trance. She turned to see a girl with a long brown braid, black, thick glasses, and a very friendly smile, pointing at the bunk nearest to the door. "That seems to be the only bunk left. You have your pick of the top or the bottom. We must be getting a cover kid later. She can take whichever one you don't want."

Mitzi smiled. "Hey. Thanks. I'm Mitzi, by the way."

The girl laughed to herself, and Mitzi suddenly felt hot in her face again. "We *all* know who you are!" she said. "I was a bit nervous coming to talk to you, but you looked a little bit lost so I thought I should help. It's my second year here and I remember how it all felt like too much at first. You doing alright, Mitzi Clark?"

Mitzi's insides crumbled a bit. She didn't want everyone knowing who she was. She would much prefer to blend in and get used to things slowly, but everything at camp so far was pointing to her goals of anonymity being an impossibility.

"I'm fine," Mitzi said flatly as she plopped her

bags onto the top mattress. "I think I'll take this bunk. Thank you, urm…what is your name?"

"Oh, sorry, yeah. My name's Anya, and that over there," she said, pointing to a pretty girl with freckles and bright red curly hair, "is my bestie, Charlotte. But we call her Charlie. You come find one of us if you need help with anything."

"Okay, thanks! I'm really looking forward to…" Her voice trailed off as Anya turned and yelled hello to another friend across the room, before Mitzi mumbled, "Okay. Never mind, then."

"Most of the girls here are like that. All sugar and not much spice," a throaty voice came from the bottom bunk next to Mitzi's.

"Oh, hey." Mitzi tried to hide the surprise in her voice. "I'm sorry I didn't see you there."

"That's because I'm not clucking around like all these chickens," the girl said, propping her head on the hand being held up by her elbow, her purple and black streaked hair half covering her face. "Name's Seph. And I already know who you are so you can save you breath."

"Seph?" Mitzi asked. "That's a cool name."

"It's short for Persephone. But that's a mouthful, so I go by Seph."

"Is this your first year here, too?" Mitzi asked even though she was pretty sure that it wasn't.

"My third year, and I just want to get this summer over with."

"Why? What's so bad about it?"

"It's not that. Well, I mean most of these girls are simple and annoying, but mostly I just want to be home with my friends. And my boyfriend. You have a boyfriend back home?"

"Nah. I'm not really interested in having one either, to be honest," Mitzi lied, as her mind flooded with images of Trent, wondering if he was settling into his cabin any easier than she was.

"Whatever," Seph groaned as she rolled over onto her other side. Apparently, she was done talking to Mitzi.

Mitzi climbed up to her bunk and stretched out on top of her camp-issued blankets, covering her head with her camp-issued pillow, trying hard not to think of home. *Nothing feels comfortable. Things feel so unknown and chaotic. Everyone else seems so familiar and at ease. Things would be so much better if Rose was my bunkmate.*

Mitzi was trying hard to not imagine the 'cover', that would be arriving later, and sleeping beneath her, to be a horrible and snotty girl. "Just try to stay positive." She sighed into her pillow. "Everything is going to be fine."

***

A sudden buzzing on her wrist snapped Mitzi awake. She must have dozed off and now her heart was pounding as she fought to shake the fogginess out of her brain. She looked down at her buzzing smartwatch and the words, **Picnic at the Pavilion** were flashing in bright red letters. Puzzled, and still not quite awake, she brought the watch close to her face to see if she could figure out how to get the buzzing to stop.

"You just have to tap it twice," she heard Seph's voice from below. "It's annoying at first, but you'll get used to it."

Mitzi gave the watch face a double tap and the buzzing stopped. "Thanks," she said. "That scared the crap out of me."

"Really?" Seph said as she stood up and walked over to the edge of Mitzi's bunk. "The great hunter, Mitzi Clark was frightened by a little buzz?"

Mitzi was taken aback. Her face crumpled into confusion, not knowing if this girl was being serious or just messing with her.

"Oh, relax." Seph rolled her eyes dramatically. "I'm only screwing with ya. Come on. I'll walk with you down to the pavilion."

Mitzi's shoulders relaxed. "My friend Rose is probably waiting outside for me, to walk down, if you...

"Oh whatever," Seph interrupted. "Go find your friend then."

"I was only gonna say," Mitzi said, confused by Seph's strange behavior, "that maybe the three of us could head down to the picnic *together*. You could show us both around?"

Seph's pale skin flushed a deep red. "That sounds good. As long as she's not a chicken like you...*buzz buzz.*"

"Rose?" Mitzi laughed. "Nope. She's a sarcastic drama queen like you. You're gonna love her."

Chapter Six

"Who the hell is this?" Rose yelled playfully at Mitzi and Seph as they approached her out front of cabin four.

"Hey, Rose," Mitzi said, nodding her head. "This is my new friend, Seph. It's her third year here, and she said she would give us the camp rundown. Seph, this is Rose."

"Hey girl," Rose said, and smiled at Seph warmly. "Love the hair. It has great vibes."

"Thanks," she said, returning the smile. "Let's get down to pavilion before all the good food's gone. I am starving."

"Yep," Rose said, elbowing Mitzi as the three started walking across the large field toward the busy pavilion. "She's cool."

"All right then," Seph cleared her throat, "let me give you two the quick run down."

"Camp STASH has four regular cabins. Cabins one and four are for the girls, and Cabin two and three are for the boys. *Except* for the Seniors. They have a co-ed cabin way on the other side of camp. The staff cabin is in the woods right behind our cabins, just so you know."

Rose's eyes bulged with excitement. "The seniors are just over there with each other? Boys *and* girls? No adults?"

"Crazy, right?" Seph said. "They have the building split in two, though. Girls are upstairs and the boys are down. Each floor has a captain, too."

"A captain?" Mitzi asked.

"Yep," Seph said. "The third-year campers vote on it at the end of every year. It's just like another stupid popularity contest. Like prom queen.

Every year, it's the prettiest and most popular girl and the dumbest dude. Bleh. Anyway, they are the ones that are responsible for the house and they report directly to Ms. Linda. The boss lady."

"Is that the same Linda that checked us into camp?" Rose asked.

"The one and only," Seph said. "I heard her yell your name and blow your cover. What a jerk."

"I think that everyone in camp heard her," Mitzi said, "but I somehow feel like she did it on purpose, too."

"She has a reputation for blabbing every one's personal business all over camp, so watch what you say around her," Seph said as they arrived at the back of the long line of campers waiting for food. "Oh man, that chicken smells amazing!"

"Heck yeah, it does," Rose said. "So who are the Senior Captains this year? Do you know them?"

Seph stood on her tiptoes to look over the line in front of them. "You see that gorgeous blonde over there by the first picnic table? That's Bella. She's a total snob. Acts like she's God's gift to the world."

"Yep," Mitzi said. "She was actually on our flight over."

"Her sisters are in my cabin and they seem alright so far, though," Rose added. "And what about the boy?"

"That's Jeremy," Seph said. "He's actually pretty cool."

"Huh?" Rose asked. "Care to elaborate?"

"See that guy sitting all the way at the back corner table all by himself?" She nodded toward the table. "That's Jeremy. He's always quiet, sticks to himself most of the time."

Mitzi curiously watched the boy that was so rude to her earlier, sitting alone in the corner, spooning mouthfuls of mashed potatoes into his mouth without looking up from his plate at all. "He was pretty rude to me earlier," she said.

"Was he a jerk to you?" Seph raised her voice. "What's up with that? I bet he has a thing for you. Boys are so weird."

Rose lifted her hand into the air in protest. "Now wait just a minute, Seph. You said that the campers vote every year to decide who the captain will be. That guy really isn't cute at all, and he sure the heck doesn't seem to be popular. So then what's the deal?"

"I think it was a prank," she said, shrugging her shoulders. "All the guys agreed to vote for the least popular kid or something, to be jerks. I don't understand it, at all. Like I said before, boys are weird."

"That's messed up," Rose mumbled.

"Yeah, it is," Mitzi agreed as a sadness ripped through her.

She hated to see anyone singled out in a bad way. *Maybe that's why he was such a grouch. Maybe he was just sick of other people making him feel small. It would suck to be an outcast. But then why was he so rude to me?*

They slowly made it to the front of the food line and after the strange and unusual new task of scanning in their smart watches, the three loaded their trays up with BBQ chicken, cornbread, beans, and ziti. The food looked and smelled amazing, which was a huge relief to Mitzi after dealing with a school year of super nasty cafeteria lunches.

The trio found a table with just a few campers at one end, and sat down to eat. They ate without talking and finished just as Ms. Linda appeared from out of nowhere, stood on a bench in the front of the pavilion, and started yelling.

"Campers! Campers! Settle down now!"

The pavilion suddenly became very quiet. It happened so quickly and it surprised Mitzi that she could even hear someone set their fork down.

"Welcome new campers, and welcome back returning campers, to SHUT's Training Academy for Supernatural Hunters, also known as Camp STASH!"

A cheer rang out, and a now smiling Ms. Linda raised her hand in the air, instantly quieting the crowd.

"Senior Campers, listen up! There will be absolutely no Midnight Mayhem this year! I mean it. There will be serious consequences for any who disobeys this rule!"

A soft chuckle erupted from a few of the tables as Mitzi and Rose both turned to Seph in search of an explanation.

"I'll tell you later," she whispered urgently.

"Enough of that now," Linda snapped at the still laughing campers, who quieted quickly. "Classes and Jobs start tomorrow. As always, your watches will alert you as to where to go and when. You must scan into all classes, activities, and jobs. Failure to do so will result in extra unpaid duties.

"The cover students will arrive shortly before midnight. Please make them feel welcome."

Mitzi smiled at the thought of seeing Finn. She could hardly wait to hear about his cover camp and introduce him to Seph.

"You are on free time until lights out at 11. You may check out the beach, the marina, see where the class cabins are, come down to the fire pit to hang out with your friends, or stop by the snack shack. You may also return to your cabins if you wish. Just be sure to scan in! Be safe, be smart, and see you for

Monday breakfast tomorrow."

She stepped down from the bench and disappeared around the side of the pavilion just as quickly as she came. The large space grew louder and louder by the second, filled with declarations and the plans of about a hundred energetic campers.

Mitzi and Rose both turned to face Seph. Rose looked as though she would burst. "Girl, what the heck is Midnight Mayhem and where do I sign up?" she blurted.

Chapter Seven

"Calm yourself." Seph laughed. "It's just this stupid camp tradition. Every year Linda makes the same speech, and every year at midnight on the first night of camp, the seniors plaster the staff cabin with toilet paper, confetti, and window paint. Then they have an unauthorized bonfire and howl at the moon at midnight. That's about all."

"Sounds pretty fun to me," Mitzi said.

"Sure," Seph said, shrugging. "Until tomorrow morning when Linda pretends that she doesn't know who made the mess and the first-year campers are made to clean it all up."

"Well, that's some BS right there," Rose grumbled.

"So, you had to clean up your first year?" Mitzi

asked. "How bad was it?"

"There are worse things," she said. "But yeah. It kind of sucks. Why don't we head out of here and see if we can get into some mayhem of our own?"

A mischievous smile flashed across Rose's face. "Heck yes! Now you're talking."

Mitzi's shoulders dropped. She didn't want to start her camp experience off by getting into trouble. She wanted to keep her head down and just blend in. She looked at her two friends, silently wishing they were a bit less adventurous.

"How about you show us around, instead?" Mitzi asked. "Give us the big tour?"

"Fine, fine." Seph sighed. "But if we are gonna be friends, Mitzi Clark, I will be expecting a little more gumption from you."

"She can be a bit of a stick-in-the-mud," Rose added. "I'm glad I will finally have a partner in crime."

Mitzi watched as the two girls laughed before giving each other a fist bump. She tried not to let Rose's comments get to her, but was feeling bruised. Why would Rose, of all people, say she was a stick-in-the-mud? *Wasn't it me that pushed Rose to investigate all the clues at the farmhouse in the first place? She would never even be in SHUT at all if it wasn't for me! Why is she trying so hard to impress Seph?*

But as the three got up to take the camp tour, Mitzi decided to let it go. Rose was her best friend and everyone says dumb stuff once in a while. But Mitzi's brain was swirling and she couldn't stop overthinking. *But then again, maybe Rose is right. Maybe I am being lame.* That's when she got an idea.

"I actually have an idea of some trouble we can get into," Mitzi blurted, stopping the two in their tracks.

"Oh, do tell," Rose said, crossing her arms.

"I was thinking it would be kind of cool to introduce Seph to the Finster when he gets here, and welcome him properly, instead of waiting until breakfast to see him," Mitzi said smugly.

"Oh, that's good, girl," Rose said, uncrossing her arms and bouncing up and down with excitement. "What do you say, Seph?"

Seph looked Mitzi slowly up and down, with a look of admiration plastered on her face. "I say, that sounds like an epic idea. Dang, Mitzi! Maybe you are an evil genius after all."

"Maybe," Mitzi said proudly, "but we have some planning to do. I may like breaking the rules for a bit of fun, but I sure as heck don't want to get caught."

"Same," said Rose.

"No problem," Seph said. "How about we

walk around camp and come up with some ideas before we hit our cabins, and work out the details."

And that's just what they did.

Chapter Eight

The plan was set. The distant hum of an airplane alerted Mitzi that it was time to get out of bed and, as doubt flooded her brain, she glanced over the edge of her bed and saw Seph sitting up and staring her way.

"You ready?" Seph whispered.

Mitzi nodded.

"Don't forget to leave your watch behind," Seph said as she stood and stretched. "Hopefully, this is gonna work."

Mitzi climbed down from her bed as quietly as she could but the metal frame was creaking, sending worry pulsating through her with every step. Once her feet were firmly planted, she looked around the room, grateful that no one seemed to have awakened from the commotion. Without a word, the two stepped out into the cold, dark night and raced to the bathrooms.

"What took you guys so long?" Rose said, shivering with a giant smile on her face as she and Seph scanned themselves inside followed by a watch-less Mitzi. "I'm freezing!"

"You'll live," Seph said. "Rose, take off your watch. We can each stash them behind a toilet. Then the fun starts."

"I still don't get why I left my watch back in the cabin," Mitzi said.

"Because," Seph sounded annoyed, "if two of us are gone for a long time from the same cabin, it would raise suspicion!"

"Why are *you* worried?" Rose added. "If they *are* watching the scans, then you are still in bed."

"Enough talking!" Seph snapped as she put

the watches behind a toilet. "We gotta move! We need to scan out of here within the next fifteen minutes if we are gonna pull this off. You both ready to run?"

Mitzi was not ready. Her heart was thumping and her hands were shaking but she couldn't change her mind now. "Ready."

"Let's do this," Rose said.

They took off running as fast as they could along the tree line toward the main hall. They figured the best place to surprise Finn would be after he checked in, on his walk from reception to his cabin.

"Hey look, you two!" Seph continued to run as she pointed at the large field to the left of them. "The seniors are starting the mayhem!"

Mitzi could just make out a dozen or so people running across the field and toward the cabins. She was comforted by the fact that the seniors' mayhem, would be a great diversion as they approached the back corner of the building.

They crept quietly to the front corner to get a better vantage point of the door. They watched as pairs of cover students started trickling out into the night and toward the cabins. But no Finn.

"Where the heck is this friend of yours?" Seph whispered frantically.

Mitzi shrugged her shoulders just as the door opened again and out came Finn, holding his schedule firmly in his hand and taking in his first full view of Camp STASH.

"PSSSTT!" Rose tried to get his attention before whisper-shouting, "Finny!"

A startled Finn strained his eyes in their direction. "Rose?"

"Shhhh. Keep it down, dork!" Rose scolded and waved him toward them. "Get your butt over here!"

Finn looked around to make sure no one was watching before doing as he was told. "What are you guys doing here? And who the heck is this?"

"We wanted to sneak out and surprise you." Mitzi giggled, but then a puzzled look took over her face. "Where are your glasses? Can you even see anything?"

"Yeah, I can see. Dad finally took me to get contacts. You guys are freakin' nuts. You could have just said hello in the morning you know."

Rose punched him in the arm. "That's the thanks we get for trying to make you feel welcome, huh?"

"Ow!" Finn rubbed his arm. "Thank you for the nice surprise, geesh."

"Hey, I'm Seph. I bunk with Mitzi in Cabin Four," she said. "Are you in Two or three?"

"I'm in Cabin Two," he said.

Mitzi was starting to get worried that they were taking too long. "Let's get him there and get you both scanned out of the bathroom. We are taking too long!"

"Scanned out of the bathroom?" Finn asked. "What on earth are you talking about?"

"We'll explain later, but now we've gotta move!" Seph grabbed Finn's elbow and took off with him, running toward the cabins via the tree line. The four arrived breathless and sweating, at the front door of Cabin Two just a few short minutes later and Seph wordlessly pointed to the front door.

"Goodnight, you weirdos," Finn said. "See you in the morning, and thanks for the welcome."

Mitzi and Rose waved Finn a quick goodbye before running after Seph, who was already halfway back to the bathrooms.

Seph scrambled to retrieve the watches from behind the toilets and scanned them at the door, in a quick flurry of movements. "We just might pull this off! Now remember, Rose, walk a normal pace back to your cabin and if anyone stops you, tell them you've been in the bathroom with a stomach ache."

"Got it!" she said. "Goodnight, ladies."

"Goodnight, Rose!" Mitzi said before turning to Seph. "We had better get back ourselves!"

"Absolutely!" she said, but a mischievous grin crept over her face again. "What do you say we take a short detour and see what damage the seniors are doing to the staff house?"

Mitzi didn't want to push it. She felt like she was playing with fire already but didn't want Seph to think she was dull and boring. "Okay, but let's make it quick. I really don't want to get caught!"

"That a girl. We won't get caught," she said

firmly as she turned off the path, into the woods and toward the staff house.

They were only a short way into the woods before they could hear voices, chatting and laughing, coming from just ahead. Mitzi's heart raced with excitement and she thought the whole idea of Midnight Mayhem was pretty cool. As they moved in closer, they could see the house was plastered in toilet paper and silly string. A few seniors were still busy soaping windows and a few others spreading toothpaste on the doorknob.

"I don't get it," Mitzi whispered. "The staff have to know they are there. Why don't they just come out and stop them?"

"Strange, I know," Seph agreed. "Most traditions are weird if you think about it long enough."

She had a point. Mitzi couldn't help but to

think about Christmas and the absurdity of a fat man dressed in a red suit, shimmying his way down a chimney, to give kids presents. *Yep. Weird.*

"Come on, let's go," Seph mumbled. "This is lame, and I am getting tired."

But as she turned to head back, she suddenly threw up her arm, stopping Mitzi in her tracks. She brought her finger to her lips and then pointed toward the path in the other direction before silently bringing her finger to her ear.

Mitzi stood as still as possible and could barely make out a soft conversation. Cupping her hand to her ear, she leaned forward but still couldn't make out what was being said, much less who was saying it. She mouthed to Seph, "Let's get closer," and the two tiptoed through the woods as quietly as possible, trying not to step on sticks and give away their presence. After a few stressful moments, they stopped to listen again and this time, Mitzi could make out a heated conversation between two men. They still couldn't see them, but Mitzi didn't want to risk moving any closer.

"I mean it, John!" an angry and annoyed voice snapped. "We are in it, and it's far too late in the game to back out now."

"I'm not trying to back out!" the other man said. "Would you just listen to me, please?"

"I am done listening! The operation will proceed as planned. It's too late for changes. There's too much involved!"

"Fine." The voice was flat and deep. "But if I go down for this, I'm taking you with me."

"We will be fine. We will be long gone before the real trouble begins."

"I really hope you are right."

"I am. This Friday night. Right here. Got it?"

"Got it."

All Mitzi could hear now was retreating footsteps, so she bravely took a few more steps forward, trying to get a view of at least one of the men before it was too late. But by the time she could see the path in the darkness, they were gone.

Chapter Nine

The morning came too quickly. Mitzi had spent the rest of her night tossing and turning in her bed, consumed with the mysterious conversation she and Seph had overheard in the woods during their little adventure. As she crawled down from the top bunk, she let out a sharp gasp, startled to see a girl sleeping in the bed below her.

The girl sat up in bed, awakened by Mitzi's sound off. She had short brown hair that was poking out in a million directions and striking green eyes. Her eyes darted around the room and Mitzi couldn't help but feel bad for the girl. She looked so nervous.

"Good morning," Mitzi said softly. "I'm sorry if I startled you. I forgot you were coming. I'm Mitzi, and it's my first year here."

"I'm Millie. It's my first year here, too. I was recruited by SHUT because of my archery skills. At least that's what they told me."

"Archery, huh?" Mitzi was impressed. "That's pretty amazing. My best friends Rose and Finn were recruited, too. I'll introduce you to them later. I come from a SHUT family."

"She comes from SHUT royalty, actually," Seph said as she sat up in bed, rubbing her face. "Her father is the head of the northeast division."

"Oh, wow," Millie said, now staring at Mitzi with wide eyes. "I didn't even know this whole world existed until a few weeks ago. My parents think I am at a place called 'The Wilderness Survival Training Facility for Exceptional Youth,' in the hills of West Virginia for the summer. I'm still just trying to figure out why they picked me."

"You should consider yourself special," Seph

said. "Only a handful of non-SHUT kids are worthy enough for the invite. Plus, archery is pretty badass. I happen to be quite the archer myself. We must need you or else you wouldn't be here. Name's Seph, by the way."

Millie nodded at Seph and stood up. She was a tiny thing! She was at least a full foot shorter than Mitzi, who couldn't help but stare at her.

"I know, I know," Millie said defensively. "I'm short. I'm skinny. I'm tiny. Let's move on."

Mitzi could feel her cheeks burn. She didn't mean to stare. She glanced over at Seph, who seemed to pick up on her embarrassment. "Well, I'm tall, obnoxious, and a bit crazy," Seph said before pointing at Mitzi, "and she's famous, freckly, and a bit dull."

Seph winked at Mitzi, and the three laughed, the tension in the air melting away. The cabin around them started filling up with the scratchy voices of waking campers and the bustle of them getting ready for the first day. Mitzi's watch started buzzing and notified her that it was twenty minutes until breakfast.

Seph stood and scratched her head. "You can scramble to get a shower now, but I take mine after dinner. Less of a wait. I usually get dressed and stop at the bathroom on my way to breakfast, but you two can do what you want."

Millie scrambled to gather her clothes and toiletries. "I'm gonna go shower now. I'd rather miss breakfast than a morning shower. I don't feel awake without one!"

While Millie went out the door in a flash, Mitzi decided to take Seph's advice. A shower could wait. She just wanted to get to breakfast quickly, and tell Rose and Finn about the overheard conversation in the woods, surprised that Seph hadn't brought it up yet.

"So, what do you think that whole thing was about last night?" Mitzi asked.

"Oh, who knows," she said. "Nothing we need to worry about."

"Are you serious?" Mitzi said, her voice raising. "He said 'we'd be gone before the real trouble begins!'. Don't you think that sounds like something to worry about?"

Seph rubbed her face and blew out a sigh. "Listen, Mitzi, it was probably just a couple of obnoxious senior boys, making some kind of prank or something. Don't get your panties in a wad. Not everything needs saving."

"I think you're wrong," Mitzi said, crossing her arms. "That was an important conversation we overheard. A dangerous one. I can feel it in my gut."

"The only thing my gut is feeling is hungry. So if you don't mind, I'm going to go snag some breakfast."

Mitzi stood there dumbfounded as Seph pulled on a pair of jeans, slipped on some flip flops, and without another word, walked passed Mitzi and out the door.

"At least I know that Finn and Rose will take me seriously," Mitzi mumbled under her breath as she grabbed herself some clean clothes. Her mind churned as she changed, wishing that she saw the faces of those men in the dark. But then again, maybe Seph was right. It may have been nothing.

It didn't sound like nothing, though.

Just as Mitzi expected, Rose was waiting for her right outside the cabin, looking happy and awake, the opposite of how Mitzi was currently feeling.

"Dang, girl!" Rose said. "You, my friend, are

lookin' a bit beat down if you don't mind my sayin' so. Are you okay?

"No. I mean, yes. I mean, no. It's just that…"

"Spit it out. What happened?"

Mitzi explained to Rose exactly what happened in the woods and even told her about the new girl Millie, and Seph's reaction to the whole thing.

"I mean, it's weird," Rose said, shrugging her shoulders, "but I think I'm with Seph on this one. It was probably either some personal drama with the teachers, or a couple of seniors planning the *ultimate* prank."

Mitzi deflated. "I guess *maybe* it was nothing. But I think we need to *at least* keep our guards up, and our eyes open for anything strange."

"Plus," Rose continued, "I don't think there is a safer place in the whole world than this island.

Think about it, we are in the middle of nowhere, surrounded by water, and only a handful of people within the organization even know where we are. What real trouble could we even be in?"

"Things change," Mitzi said as the girls started walking to breakfast. "We thought the Den was impenetrable, and the Covenant Cube was perfectly safe and then look at what happened. It wasn't safe at all, and now the Vamps and werewolves are in possession of their deadliest weapon. Only the Shadow Men need the last vial and together they can release the ultimate weapon on the world. You know, the Dark Trinity? What about *that*?"

"True," Rose said. "But I really think you are being paranoid about *this*. Camp has nothing to do with all that nonsense. Just relax."

Mitzi winced, stung by her best friend's words. "Fine. I'll drop it. Just promise if you hear, or see anything strange at all..."

"You'll be the first to know!" Rose interrupted.

Chapter Ten

"I promise, Mitzi," Finn said as he shoveled his last forkful of eggs into his mouth. "I will keep my eyes open for anything weird."

"Thanks, Finn." Mitzi smiled and sipped her orange juice.

"Can we please move on now?" Rose whined. "I'm sick of talking about this."

Mitzi nodded and, although she was thrown off by Rose's flippant attitude about the whole thing, she sat trying to come up with something new to talk about. Relief flooded through her as Linda appeared at the front of the pavilion and stood on a bench, again, silencing the crowd in an instant.

"Good morning, Campers. Today we will begin our training schedules, but first we have some important matters to address."

A few giggles erupted from the tables in the back corner.

"It seems that sometime last night, the staff cabin was vandalized. The guilty parties have exactly 15 minutes to claim responsibility for their actions. I will be standing near the condiment table, and I suggest the guilty party comes forward."

Finn tapped Mitzi's shoulder and leaned in to whisper, "Didn't the seniors do that? I heard that they do it every year."

"Yep," Mitzi said with a roll of her eyes. "And every year, Linda pretends that she doesn't know who did it, and then makes the first-year kids clean it up. It's just a tradition."

"That's messed up," Finn said as he pulled a crumpled paper from his pocket and started trying to smooth it out on the table. "Anyway, do we have any classes together?"

Rose leaned in to take a closer look at his schedule.

"Looks like we all have HAC together, second period," Rose said. "Then you have weapons and survival with Mitzi last period, but you are alone for the other two."

Mitzi watched Finn's face drop. "Don't feel bad, Finny, Rose and I only have one other class together, too."

"Better than none." He shrugged and stood with his empty tray. "Guess I will head off to Pharma class."

Mitzi stood. "We can still walk together, you know. The class cabins are all next to each other."

"That's good," he said, sounding relieved, "cuz I have no idea where I am supposed to go."

Just as Rose was starting to stand and join

them, Deana D's voice came blaring over the speaker.

"No one has claimed responsibility for last night's," Deana D paused to clear her throat, continuing with a slight giggle, "*mayhem*. So it has been decided that all first-year campers are to report now to the staff house for cleanup. Your first period instructors have been advised that you will be late to class. Here is a song to kick off our first day of classes, so enjoy… and don't forget to scan in and out!"

An upbeat pop song started blaring through the speakers as a groaning Finn shook his head. "Couldn't she pick a less annoying song? It's too early for this crap."

"It's not so bad, Finn." Rose stood and grabbed her tray. "Let's get out of here, you guys. Sounds like we have some work to do."

Mitzi followed her friends to drop off their trays and then the trio slowly made their way to the staff house for the cleanup.

Cleaning up wasn't nearly as bad as Mitzi thought it would be. There were at least fifty kids there, and the whole thing only took about twenty minutes. Mitzi and Finn grabbed a bunch of toilet paper off the ground and stuffed it into a garbage bag, but there really wasn't enough work to go around. Rose didn't do anything to help but that didn't really surprise Mitzi. Rose wasn't someone who liked to get her hands dirty.

They were only a few minutes late to class, and when Rose and Mitzi walked into the RIOT cabin, with a few other first year campers, it seemed as though the class hadn't really started yet. Everyone was chatting and standing around with no teacher anywhere in sight.

After scanning in, Rose led them to an unoccupied table and they sat down, unsure of what else to do. "Where the heck is the teacher?" she asked Mitzi, who shrugged in reply.

They sat for only a few moments before the door swung open and Linda came storming in, visibly annoyed. It only took a few seconds for the other campers to realize her arrival, and the room quickly quieted as the kids scrambled to their seats.

"I know you are surprised to see me here," Linda announced. "I waited until I saw that everyone was scanned in before coming down. I'm sorry to say that Ms. Walker has taken ill and will not be teaching today, or in the near future for that matter."

No one moved an inch. Mitzi was holding her breath, hoping that Linda would not be the substitute. There was just something about her that Mitzi didn't trust. But a surge of dread spread through her as Linda continued her speech.

"It has fallen upon me to teach this course for now. I have never taught a RIOT class before. For those of you who are *new* campers, RIOT stands for Regulations, Investigations, and Operative Training, which, luckily, I happen to know a lot about. But I will need some time to prepare for our lessons. For today, you can use the rest of this session as free time. Be mindful of the other classrooms and make sure you remember to scan in and out! I will see you all in here tomorrow." And as soon as the last word came out of her mouth, she quickly turned and left the building.

"That sucks," Rose said. "I don't know why, but I don't like that lady at all."

Mitzi was glad that it wasn't just her. "I agree. There is something off about her but it looks like, for now, we're stuck with her."

"What do you want to do with the rest of our hour?" Rose asked.

"I'm open to ideas," Mitzi said. "We could check out the snack shack, or hang out in our cabin?"

"The snack shack sounds cool. Let's do that."

Mitzi and Rose scanned themselves out of the cabin and followed a small group of campers, who also seemed to be heading toward the little store. After scanning themselves in, Mitzi couldn't help but to smile as she stepped into the shop. It was much bigger than she expected from a store called "shack."

"I can't believe this," Rose exclaimed. "This is a proper store! Look, they even have a coffee station!"

Mitzi couldn't help but to smile at Rose, amused by her excitement. She did love to shop, so this store was clearly important to her.

"Yes!" Mitzi agreed. "But the real question is,

do they have peanut butter cups?"

"Well, of course we do!" Both girls turned, startled by a voice right behind them. "We have pretty much every snack and sweet you can think of."

Verna, the old woman they had met during orientation, whose arms were loaded with bags of chips, pushed passed them and started stacking the bags on the shelf.

"Can't wait until we have pay from our jobs, so we can actually shop," Rose said to Mitzi.

The woman continued stacking the chips and said, "Every camper has 20 camp coins to start off camp with. You think I would remember to tell you this stuff at orientation but I get forgetful in my old age! Why aren't you kids all in class now anyway?"

Mitzi started making herself a cup of coffee. "Ms. Walker is sick and Linda is going to take over lessons for her, starting tomorrow."

"She was fine yesterday!" the old woman said as she finished stacking the last bag of chips. "I'll have to check on her later, but for now, I better go attend to that line." She shuffled passed the girls toward the register where five campers were lined up, waiting to check out.

"I know what you are about to say, Mitzi," Rose said as she rolled her eyes.

"What?" Mitzi said as she sipped her coffee, pretending that Rose wasn't right. "I wasn't going to say anything."

Rose put her hand on her hip. "Oh come on! She was fine yesterday. I know you think that must mean something. I know you do."

"Maybe." Mitzi giggled at her friend. "But I wasn't gonna say anything about it yet."

"What do you mean *yet?*"

"I was gonna bring it up with Nurse Alex later.

See what he has to say before I assume anything suspicious is going on."

"Girl, you are insane," Rose said, nodding her head. "You really never shut that detective brain of yours off, do you?"

"Nope. I don't." Mitzi shrugged and smiled. "You getting anything? I'm gonna go check out."

"Just grabbing a couple things and I'll meet you in line," Rose said before disappearing around the corner.

Mitzi waited at the end of the line for Rose to finish her shopping and an idea came to her. By the time it was her turn to check out, she and Rose were the only two campers still in the store.

"That's one coin for the coffee," Verna told Mitzi. "Just scan your watch there, and your coin balance will show on the little screen."

"Okay," Mitzi said, doing as she was told.

"Can I ask you a strange question?"

"You can try," she said.

"Is there anyone who works here at camp named John?" Mitzi asked as Rose walked up to finally check out.

The old woman gave Mitzi a hard and suspicious look.

Rose swooped in to save her. "Are you asking about that nice pen you found?" Mitzi shot Rose a confused look as Rose kept explaining. "She found a really nice pen, engraved with the name John, and is trying to return it to its owner. Figured it must belong to a teacher. Do you know of anyone named John?"

"I had an uncle named John," she said, her face softening. "But there ain't any teachers around here named John. Not that I can think of. And I have worked here for over thirty years! Why don't you just drop it off at lost and found? If it's important, they'll get it back."

"Okay! Thanks," Mitzi said as Rose scanned in her payment.

When they got back outside, Mitzi turned to Rose. "You are brilliant! Thanks for the save in there."

"You know it, girl." Rose laughed. "But now we have another problem."

"I know," Mitzi said. "We need to figure out who this guy John is. And he sounded like a grown up, so I'd put my money on a senior."

"Exactly."

Chapter Eleven

Mitzi and Rose made it to their next class with a few moments to spare, so they waited outside for Finn, before scanning into the class cabin. Mitzi's watch started to buzz, flashing **HAC 5 MINS** just as Finn came walking toward them, looking tired and pale.

Finn looked down at his watch. "What the heck does HAC stand for again? All these acronyms are driving me nuts."

"I think it's History and Creatures," Rose said as she was pushed aside by a camper making his way to the door. But Rose wasn't one to be pushed around and wasn't having it. "Rude! You could have walked around me, you know!"

A dark haired and short boy turned around

and snapped back at Rose, "If you don't wanna get knocked over, then don't stand in front of the door, you idiot." He disappeared inside before Rose had a chance to answer back.

Rose's face curled into a snarl. "That rude son of…."

"Never mind that jerk," Finn interrupted. "All of the guys in my cabin are super rude and grouchy. I don't get it."

"To be honest, Finn," Mitzi said softly, "you are looking pretty run down yourself."

"I feel a bit off," he admitted. "I don't think I got enough sleep. Maybe that's what everyone's problem is."

"I'm sure tomorrow will be better," Mitzi said. "Let's get scanned in and find our seats. I don't want to be late."

The three managed to find seats together in

the back of the room as the other campers filed in. Mitzi watched the teacher sitting at a desk in the front, glancing up every so often, seemingly counting the students as they arrived. After a few more minutes, he stood and introduced himself as Mr. Ross and quickly dove right into the first lesson.

"Man, he isn't wasting any time, is he?" Rose whispered to Mitzi as Mr. Ross continued speaking on the importance of the History of the SHUT organization.

"Seriously," Finn joined in. "Could his voice be any duller? He's gonna put me to sleep."

Mr. Ross stopped his lesson mid-sentence and glared at Finn. "Do you have something to add to my lesson, young man?"

Mitzi held her breath as Finn squirmed in his seat. "Sorry, sir," Finn mumbled, his cheeks as red as fire.

"What was so important that you had to talk during my lesson?" Mr. Ross asked, sinking Finn deeper in his seat.

Mitzi braced herself. Knowing how tired he was, Mitzi wasn't sure if Finn was sharp enough to come up with something fast. "It's my fault!" she blurted.

Mr. Ross turned his head toward her and a slight curl of his lip made him appear entertained by Mitzi's admonition. "Oh please, do tell," he said.

Mitzi had to think up something good, and fast. "I was telling him outside before class how much I really don't like history and I was worried this class would be boring. So, after a few moments of your captivating lesson, he leaned over and said, 'See, this guy is great! Not boring at all'."

The words came out of her mouth so fast that she didn't notice Finn shaking his head, or Rose slap her hand to her face. She did, however, hear the giggles erupt from the other students in the room.

"Oh, so you think you're funny, huh?" Mr. Ross said through clenched teeth.

"No. I wasn't trying to be funny. I was…."

"Get out!" he shouted. "Don't return to my class until you learn some respect!"

"Sir, I didn't mean to…"

"NOW!"

Mitzi wanted to crawl in a hole and die. She never meant to be disrespectful. She never thought her response would come out so horribly wrong. She gathered her stuff and made the long walk to the door where she scanned herself out as the entire room silently watched. Just when she thought she couldn't get any worse, someone in the class yelled out, "Ladies and gentleman, the great Mitzi Clark."

Mitzi felt sick. She had never been so

embarrassed in her life and she didn't know what to do. She found herself a spot under a large tree, to sit down and wait for the class to end. She leaned her head back against the trunk, fighting back a pool of tears building up in her eyes. A sudden slam snapped her head forward and she was shocked to see a very angry looking Finn, stomping toward her.

"What in the heck are you doing here?" Mitzi said as he plopped himself on the ground beside her.

"I got kicked out, too."

"What on earth did *you* do?"

"Well, did you hear that jerk yell out when you left the class?"

"Yeah, so?"

"Yeah, so. So, it was that same jerk from outside, earlier. He had to be dealt with so I got up and punched him in the face." Finn shrugged like it was no big deal as he rubbed the knuckles on his right hand.

"Are you out of your mind?" Mitzi was almost shouting. "You never hit anyone. Why on earth would you hit someone?"

"Oh, come on. He had it coming. Guy's a jerk. First, he pushes Rose and then disrespects you like that?" Finn was shaking with anger.

"I mean, I get why you *wanted* to punch him," Mitzi said. "I just can't believe *you* actually did that."

Finn stood up suddenly, which caught Mitzi completely off guard as he turned to her and grumbled. "I guess it's hard to believe that lame-ass Finn is *capable* of hitting someone. Nice, Mitzi. Way to kick a guy when he's down. Screw this!" And he stormed away before Mitzi had a chance to say a word in her own defense. She just sat there as her tears rolled freely down her cheeks, unable to stop them. This was not turning out to be a good day.

It seemed like forever before the class spilled out of the cabin. Noticing the rude boy's face was red and puffy filled Mitzi with a surge of pride for Finn, followed quickly by a wave of shame for making him feel bad about it all. She never in a million years meant to belittle Finn. It's just that he had never been one to get into a physical altercation. Mitzi didn't think he avoided fights because he was scared or weak, but that he avoided them because he was smart and knew that unnecessary fighting was stupid and useless. For some reason, though, he believed that Mitzi was underestimating him, and that made her so upset.

Rose rushed straight over to where Mitzi was sitting, her eyes looking like they were about to pop out of their sockets.

"My God, girl!" she shouted.

"I know, I know," Mitzi groaned.

"First of all, I can't believe that horse crap excuse you gave to the teacher! I mean really! What in God's name were you thinking?"

"I guess, I wasn't."

"And then, Finn just runs at that kid and socks him in the eye!!!" Rose seemed to be enjoying the drama a bit too much. "What next? You both gonna burn the place to the ground?"

"Very funny, Rose, but you don't even know the worst part," Mitzi said, shaking her head. "Finn came out here, I insulted him, and then he yelled at me and stormed off."

"Seriously?" Rose asked. "What in the world is up with today?"

"You can say that again."

Chapter Twelve

Finn was nowhere to be seen at lunch. Mitzi and Rose found a seat next to Mimi and Jayde, who wouldn't stop talking about the drama of the morning.

"Still can't believe he popped him one!" Mimi said, shaking her head.

Jayde giggled and leaned toward Mitzi and Rose. "You know, he is kind of cute, too. Is he single?"

"Gross," Rose said, nodding her head behind the girls. "Why don't you ask him? He's headed this way now."

Jayde sat up straight and looked down at her tray, her face's rush of color giving away her embarrassment. Finn dropped his tray on the table between Jayde and Rose, which made her face glow even redder.

"Sorry I was a jerk to you earlier, Mitzi," he grumbled, keeping his eyes on his food in front of him.

"It's all good, Finn," Mitzi said. "I didn't mean to insult you. I actually was quite impressed and thankful that you were defending me. Just caught me off guard is all."

"To be honest, I kind of shocked myself." He turned to look at Mitzi in the eyes. He looked so tired, and Mitzi had the urge to give him a hug, but decided against it. She didn't want to risk embarrassing him again. "I don't know what came over me, really. I feel so angry today."

"Let's just start today over!" Mitzi suggested.

Rose nodded her head in agreement. "That sounds perfect. What classes do you guys have after lunch? I'm in Weapons and Survival, which means I have to go change clothes. What a pain."

"I have Pharmacology," Mitzi said. "After that, I have Weapons and Survival."

"I had Pharma first thing this morning," Finn said. "The teacher is super nice, I think you'll like her. I have RIOT after lunch, but my watch just buzzed and said class is cancelled for the day so I am on free time. Then I have WS with you, Mitz."

"Awesome," Mitzi said. "I'll do my best to not insult the teacher this time."

"And I'll try not to punch anyone." Finn laughed at himself.

"And I'll just stay amazing!" Rose added.

"What do you plan to do with your free hour, Finn?" Mitzi asked.

"I was thinking about checking out the snack shack, but I think I'll take a nap instead. I could use some quiet, I think."

Rose stood with her empty tray. "Good. Then you can finish eating and we can walk to the cabins together, so I can change into those ugly clothes."

"That'll work," Finn said, shoveling a spoonful of macaroni salad into his mouth.

Mimi, who had remained quiet until now, turned to Mitzi. "Jayde and I have Pharma next, too. Want to walk together?"

"Sure," Mitzi said, hoping the sisters wouldn't bring up the morning's events again. She was ready to move past all of that.

***

Finn was right. Mitzi really like the pharmacology teacher, Ms. Stukes. She was an older lady, maybe in her seventies, absolutely tiny (about as tall as the shortest student), and had one of those smiles that was infectious. Her voice was high-pitched and bit squeaky which somehow added to her overall appeal.

She started off the class with a rundown about what they would be learning, followed by a short tour of the large storage closet, filled from floor to ceiling with small drawers and filled with things like knotgrass powder, sheep's tears, and crushed Amethyst. After the tour, she gave a closing speech that Mitzi found both hilarious and interesting.

"So, that's about it! Now, on a serious note. Pharmacology is a science. Just because I look like an old witch, doesn't mean I am one. This isn't potions class, and the point of learning this science isn't to turn into a bullfrog, or any nonsense like that. Camp STASH is not Hogwarts. We teach pharmacology, so that as hunters, you have every tool in your arsenal, to defend yourselves, and to solve the problem without violence. Yes, sometimes we must use physical force against our enemies, but, more often than not, a tool exists within this science, that can be applied safely and effectively. Just over the last year, our SHUT forces were able to stop a major mimic infiltration, using only their brilliant ideas, and a bit of knotgrass! Imagine that!"

Ms. Stukes winked at Mitzi, apparently knowing it was her who had stopped the mimics with the knotgrass.

And although Mitzi felt a surge of embarrassment, she couldn't help but feel a rush of pride, too. Mitzi smiled back at Ms. Stukes, happy that at least one of her classes today was going to plan. She was looking forward to learning pharma, especially seeing as it had already come in handy so many times already. First with the mimics, and then healing her neighbor and friend, the very old Mr. Moore after his situation with the werewolves.

Mitzi's thoughts drifted to her family at home. She wondered if the Vampires, werewolves, and Shadow Men had made a move against SHUT yet, or if they were still sticking to the shadows…

If the last blood vile was still safe.

Mitzi was so deep in thought, in fact, that she missed the end of Ms. Stukes's speech. As she followed her fellow campers out of the cabin, she had to walk past Ms. Stukes's desk.

"I'm really looking forward to this class," Mitzi said to her.

"That's good to hear!" she said. "I think we both know that you already understand the importance of this subject, having used the practice a few times already."

"I do," Mitzi said. "Thankfully, my mother keeps an amazing inventory for us. She is really good in Pharmacology."

"Of course she is!" Ms. Stukes laughed. "I'm the one who taught her."

"That's so cool," said Mitzi, feeling even more connected to this teacher, and, more importantly, to home. "See you tomorrow, ma'am."

"Can't wait."

Chapter Thirteen

It was a bit of a rush to get to the next class on time. Mitzi had to race back to her cabin to change, and get back to the training grounds, all in fifteen minutes. She made it there with only minutes to spare, and found Finn standing alone near a tree, looking even more tired than he did at lunch.

"Man, are you okay?" Mitzi asked.

He rubbed his face, grumbling, "Just really tired," as a moose of a man pushed his way through the crowd of chatting campers and stood in the center of the field with his gigantic arms crossed and a whistle in his mouth. He was tattooed with tribal symbols and scrollwork on his entire visible body, other than his face and bald head. He blew his whistle three times in short, loud bursts, silencing the crowd immediately.

"I am Instructor Dodge," he yelled in a deep and scratchy voice. "Welcome to Weapons and Survival Training. This is the most important class you will ever take. The stuff I teach you here will help you save lives, maybe even your own. So, no fartin' around. It won't be tolerated here."

Finn caught Mitzi's eye and winked at her, which she took as a silent promise not to punch anyone.

"Today, you are gonna partner up in groups of two, and start a fire. Go!" he yelled, but no one moved.

"Do we get any matches or anything?" one student yelled out.

The instructor threw his muscular head back and laughed. "You get stranded and need a fire so you don't die. You don't have matches. This is a test to see what kind of geniuses I'm working with. Now go!"

Mitzi watched as kids scrambled off in every direction. She turned to Finn. "What's your plan? Have any ideas?"

He scratched his head. "I'll go into the woods and see what kind of dry stuff I can find. You try to think of how or what we can light it with, I guess."

"Sounds good. Hurry!" she said, noticing teams already gathered around little piles, rubbing sticks together, many yelling at each other.

"Think, Mitzi," she said to herself. She noticed a garbage can out of the corner of her eye and thought there might be something worth using in there. Certainly, there wouldn't be a pack of matches but she was stumped and it was all she could come up with.

After searching through the bin, filled mostly

with used cups and bottles and wrappers of sorts, she gave up, not find anything she could use to start a fire. Finn appeared with a big handful of tiny twigs, bark, and sticks, and set them in a small pile on the ground.

"What did you think of?" he asked her, panting from the running around.

"I couldn't come up with anything!" Mitzi whined. "Should we just do what everyone else is doing?"

"Fifteen Minutes left!" Dodge shouted. "Still looking for that fire, people!"

"No," Finn said. "That's not going to work. Everything is too damp and it will take a lot longer than fifteen minutes. Hang on, and let me think."

Mitzi sat on the ground next to Finn as he quietly looked around.

He stood up in a flash and yelled, "I got it!" as

he took off running toward a couple of campers, frantically rubbing their sticks together. His back was to Mitzi and she couldn't hear what they were saying.

A moment later, he was crouching at their own sticks, holding a pair of glasses over the pile.

"What are you doing?" Mitzi was intrigued.

"If I can concentrate the sunlight through these lenses, I just might be able to get a flame going?"

"Some kid just gave you his glasses?" Mitzi laughed.

"Yep," he said. "I had to promise to tell him how to do it, if it works, though."

Finn moved the glasses around, trying to find the best spot to get the beam to focus as small as possible. He let out a frustrated groan.

"How can we concentrate the beam more?" Mitzi said.

"That's it!" he shouted. "You're a genius! Can you find me some water? I only need a tiny bit."

Mitzi's heart was pumping with excitement. She sprang to action, running to the garbage bin that she knew had empty water bottles in. Surely, she could find one with a few drops still in it. Lucky for her, the first bottle she found had a few centimeters or so still inside.

"Just put one drop in the center of the lens," Finn said, and Mitzi did as she was told, pouring a bit into her hand and carefully letting a drop roll off her finger and into the center of the lens.

"That should do it," Finn said as he carefully positioned the glasses again, this time the sun's light forming a tiny, bright beam through the bubble of water.

Mitzi held her breath and watched as the spot the light was focused on started turning dark…

Then started to smoke…

"Come on, come on…" Finn said, so focused on the smoke that he didn't notice the crowd forming around them.

Smoke….

"We got this, Finny!" Mitzi whispered, her face inches from the sticks.

A small flame erupted and in a split second, the little pile was ablaze. The onlookers cheered and Finn nearly fell over, startled by their applause.

"Well, I'll be damned," Dodge said as he squatted near the tiny fire. "You two are the first students, in my ten years here, to accomplish the first day fire test."

Cheers erupted from the crowd again.

"What's your name, son?" Dodge said.

"Finn," he answered, looking pleased with himself.

"Good job, Mr. Finn," Dodge said. "Gonna keep my eye on you. I think you have big things coming your way."

He stood up, slapping Finn on the shoulder, and stormed off the field yelling, "Dismissed!" Some kid tapped Finn on the shoulder and held out his hand, to which Finn promptly put the glasses into it.

"Thanks, man," Finn said.

"No problem!" the boy said. "Just wish I had thought of it myself. Nice job."

"Just got lucky!" Finn said as the boy ran off.

"Lucky, my butt," Mitzi said, beaming at her friend. "You are super smart, and that was *epic*."

Finn laughed. "Honestly, I can't believe it actually worked!"

"Come on," Mitzi said as she stood and extended a hand to help Finn up. "We have almost an hour before jobs start. Wanna go grab a snack at the shack?"

"That sounds perfect." Finn stomped on the fire pile to make sure it was completely out before they left. "This day is finally turning around. Last thing I want to do is burn the place to the ground."

"Truth!" Mitzi said as she hooked her arm in Finn's and they headed off to grab some snacks before work.

Chapter Fourteen

There was nothing special about the health cabin other than the large red cross symbol hanging above the door. The three walked into the cabin precisely at 3 o'clock, and found the place empty. The room smelled slightly of band aids and rubbing alcohol, which Mitzi found strangely comforting, and two cots sat on the left side of the room, with a fabric divider between them.

There was a large desk in the back right corner, piled high with papers and next to it, a large glass-front cabinet, stuffed with supplies and bottles of sorts. Against the back wall, a dark green couch that Mitzi thought looked as old as the camp itself loomed, with holes in the arm rests and rips around most of its edges. Mitzi looked around the dimly lit room and wondered where Nurse Alex could be when a soft humming came from a closed door next to the couch.

"I think he's in there," Finn whispered, nodding toward the door.

As if on cue, the door creaked open and Nurse Alex, stepped out of the room and stopped suddenly, startled by the three of them standing there.

"I didn't hear you three come in! Surely, it can't be three o'clock already," he said.

"According to our watches, it is," Mitzi said with a slight laugh.

"You know," Nurse Alex said, walking around to his desk, "I forget I am wearing mine half of the time and there are no clocks anywhere!"

Finn shrugged his shoulders. "I know they use these to track the campers; I guess it shouldn't be a surprise that they keep tabs on the staff, too."

"You would think they would trust us more," he said. "Anyway, why don't you three take a seat on the couch. It's old but it won't bite. Promise."

Rose took a hard look at the green couch and frowned. "If you're sure. But if that thing bites me, I'm suing."

Nurse Alex laughed. He laughed a bit longer than seemed normal, and Mitzi caught Finn's eye, whose bewildered look confirmed that his over reaction was a bit on the strange side.

"So, Nurse Alex," Rose said, sitting down on the very edge of the cushion.

"Please, guys, call me Alex. We will be spending way too much time together to be so formal," he said.

"Okay. So, Alex," Rose said, "what exactly are we going to be doing around here?"

He let out another long laugh, and by the look

on her face, even Rose was taken back by how over-the-top it seemed.

"There isn't much to do at all. Might have some filing once in a while, but otherwise, I just wanted to hang out and hear about your adventures, truth be told. Every year I get assigned two kids, and it's so boring. This year, I made a special request for the three of you. I never thought they would do it, but I've been putting in for a transfer for three years now, that they keep denying. I think they gave me my way this time to shut me up."

"Why do you want a transfer?" Mitzi asked. "You don't like it here?"

He stared at her for a moment before answering, which made Mitzi uncomfortable. "It's not that I don't like it," he said. "I just am a bit bored. I spend the summer stuck on the island taking care of boo boos and scraped knees. The rest of the year,

I'm assigned to a country clinic, and I'm lucky if I see ten patients a month. It's very monotonous and it feels like a giant waste of my skills."

"That does suck," Rose said. "You would think they would put you someplace else, if that's what you really want."

"Oh, kids, SHUT isn't as great as they appear. You'll see. They have a few really powerful people," he said, glaring strangely at Mitzi through sad eyes, "but the rest of us are just pawns, and they use us however they want. You will see."

Mitzi was uncomfortable again. She didn't know what to say, and the room was completely quiet now. She glanced at Finn, who shrugged his shoulders, and then at Rose, who was looking down at her hands.

"Maybe you'll get lucky this year and we will have a big outbreak of illness," Mitzi said, trying her best to sound lighthearted.

"Doubt it," he said. "No one ever gets sick here. Except for that nasty stomach bug three years ago."

"Oh, come on," Rose said. "You've already had one patient this year."

Nurse Alex shot Rose a puzzled look. "I haven't had any patients yet this year."

"Ms. Walker hasn't come to see you?" Mitzi asked. "Linda said she is sick and may be out for several days."

"Oh...oh...yeah," he stumbled to speak. "I was, I mean, I thought you were only talking about students. Yeah; she is sick. Anyway, enough about me. Why don't you three tell me all about your most recent adventures with the Covenant Cube?! I am growing sick of all this camp talk."

The three looked at each other with blank

expressions. Mitzi was unsure of what she should say.

"I don't think we are really allowed to talk about that stuff," Rose said.

"Yeah," Finn said. "We were told not to talk about the Covenant Cube."

Mitzi watched as Nurse Alex's face fell, and it suddenly occurred to her that this may be the perfect opportunity to get info out of him.

"Oh, come on, guys," she said. "I'm sure Alex knows all about it, anyway. Isn't that right, Alex?"

"Pretty much," he said with a nervous chuckle. "I mean, I know that the northeast Den was infiltrated by someone inside, and that the Covenant Cube was stolen and left in the open."

"Yes, that's right," Mitzi said.

"I also know that the Vampires and werewolves were able to steal their blood vials, but the shadow man's blood is still safely located in

SHUT's possession."

"Good thing, too," Finn said. "We would all be doomed if the dark trinity was on the loose."

"True, yes," Alex said. "I just hope they can keep the last vial safe. I mean, where are they even keeping it, now that the Den has been compromised?"

There it was.

Mitzi's suspicions were correct. He was trying to get info out of them. But *why?* She made up a quick lie to throw him off track.

"My dad said they moved it to the southern station, until the new storage facility is built." She could feel Finn and Rose staring at her as she spoke. "They moved it down there the night before we came to camp, in the middle of the night, under heavy guard. But I don't think I was supposed to say anything about it, so please don't tell anyone."

"The southern station, huh?" he said, raising his eyebrows. "Never would have guessed that. And don't worry, you can trust me."

"I'm sure we can," Mitzi said through a fake smile. "That's pretty much the only interesting thing that happened, and you seem to know most of it anyway. I could tell you about the time Finn's bloody nose tissue was used by a mimic and…"

A speaker crackled from the corner of the room, interrupting Mitzi mid-sentence. Deana D's voice came blaring through the room. "Nurse Alex, you are needed at the training field for an ankle injury. Nurse Alex, field, ankle injury."

"Of all the dang luck," Alex grumbled. "Looks like I'll have to hear about that nose bleed later. Which one of you wants to come with me on this ankle call?"

Mitzi looked at Rose and Finn, silently wishing

one of them would volunteer, and was happy when Rose stood up and said, "I'll go."

Alex smiled. "Great. You two can wait here. I'll grab my bag and the ice packs out of the cooler. We can take the golf cart. It's around the back of the building."

"Can I drive?" Rose asked.

"Sure," he said, but then grimaced. "Do you even know how to drive?"

"No, she doesn't!" Finn yelled, and Mitzi couldn't help but laugh.

"Fun ruin-er!" Rose snapped back with a giant smile on her face.

Alex made quick work of grabbing his supplies, and he and Rose were off on their ankle rescue.

Mitzi and Finn sat quietly until they heard the hum of the golf cart pulling away.

"What on earth was that all about?" Finn asked. "The southern station? You know they moved it to the…"

"Shhh," she said. "We don't know who is listening."

"What?" Finn said, clearly confused.

"Isn't it obvious, Finn?" Mitzi whispered.

Finn shook his head.

"Think, Finn. He requested us and now he has a bunch of questions. It's a bit strange."

"Mitzi, you're dreaming all this stuff up! There is no mystery here."

"I think there is, Finn. And I think Nurse Alex is involved somehow. Think about it. He's fishing for information, he doesn't like it here, and clearly has issue with SHUT."

"A lot of people don't like their jobs, Mitzi," Finn said, rolling his eyes. "It doesn't mean they are secretly plotting to take down the world."

"You are being a jerk," Mitzi said defensively. "I never said he was plotting to take down the world."

"Well, then what nefarious act do you think he is involved in then?" Finn asked.

"I'm not sure," Mitzi said, biting her nails, deep in thought. "But I plan to find out. You don't think it was weird the way he acted when I said that Ms. Walker was sick?"

Finn quietly considered her words. "Yeah, I guess that was a bit odd, but, Mitzi, he seems like a pretty cool guy and it doesn't seem like you have much to go on here."

"Maybe not," Mitzi said. "But I think that conversation we overheard in the woods shouldn't be ignored. I think one of the men might have been Alex. Now we just need to figure out who John is."

"Good luck with that," Finn grumbled. "I think I'm gonna sit this one out, Mitzi."

"That's fine," Mitzi said, feeling bruised by his disloyalty. "I'll get to the bottom of it, with or without you."

The two sat in an angry silence for the next twenty minutes and Mitzi was relieved when she finally heard the golf cart returning.

Alex was the first to enter the room and went straight to the cabinet to put his supplies away, followed by Rose, who was finishing a story.

"…and my parents have no idea where I am. They think I'm off at some regular summer camp."

"That's crazy!" Alex said, returning to where Mitzi and Finn were sitting. "You're a cover kid, too, aren't you, Finn?"

"Yep," Finn said flatly. "My parents needed the whole fake camp experience to fool them, though."

"Seems like such a waste of resources to me," Alex said, shaking his head. "Wouldn't it just make more sense if we let the public know the truth about the non-humans?"

"I don't know about that," Mitzi said. "People seem to overreact to the simplest of stuff. I don't think it would go over too well if they knew that Vampires and demons were living among us."

"Maybe not." He shrugged.

"What happened with the ankle situation?" Finn asked.

"It was actually a fight!" Rose said, bubbling from the drama of it all. "One third year camper slapped another camper and he fell over a bench and cracked his ankle on a rock on the way down."

"Just a bad bruise," Alex added. "Another boo boo."

Mitzi caught Finn's eye. "Seems like a lot of fighting so early into camp. Is that normal?"

Finn rolled his eyes.

"Boys fight," Alex said. "Anyway, your shift is almost over if you three want to scan out. I have a headache, so I'd like to catch a nap if you're cool with that."

"Works for me," Rose said as Finn and Mitzi stood up from the old couch.

"See you tomorrow then," Mitzi added as the three left the cabin, scanning themselves out along the way.

Once outside, Mitzi looked down at her watch. "It's about thirty minutes until the Tech meetup. What do you guys want to do?"

"Want to go grab a snack at the shack?" Rose asked.

"You guys do your own thing. I'm heading to

my cabin for a break," Finn said as he turned and walked away without further explanation.

"What the heck is his problem?" Rose asked.

"He's annoyed with me because I have a feeling something bad is about to go down at camp and he disagrees. Thinks I am imagining things." Mitzi shrugged her shoulders and could feel emotion building inside of her. She hated that things weren't right between them.

"Oh boy, here we go again." Rose chuckled, but put her arm around Mitzi. "What bad thing is coming our way now, Mitzi Clark?"

"Let's head to the snack shack and I'll tell you all about it."

Chapter Fifteen

Tech meetup took place in the same main cabin the orientation had been in. All the campers sat cross-legged on the floor and a giant white screen was hanging on the wall, at the far side of the room. Mitzi watched, from her seat on the floor between Finn and Rose, as Linda nervously paced underneath the screen, looking down at her watch every few seconds. The room was strangely quiet, which always seemed to be the case in Linda's presence. Rain started drumming down on the roof, creating an eerie soundtrack to the scene unfolding.

After another five minutes of nothing but the raindrops, Linda looked down at her watch for the one hundredth time before turning to address the crowd.

"It seems as though Mr. Bell will not be able to join us for his Tech time this evening. I will release you all for now and we will reconvene tomorrow for the first lesson." She walked straight down the middle of the room, the campers sliding out of her way in swift, nervous movements. She never missed a step, and the room remained quiet until the door slammed shut behind her.

Mitzi turned to Finn as the chatter around her started building. "Now do you think something may be going on?"

Mitzi was shocked as Finn rolled his eyes and stood up and said, "No, actually. I think you are ridiculous," before storming off through the crowds.

Flabbergasted and pushing down her hurt feelings, Mitzi turned to Rose. "What in the world? You are getting what I am talking about, right? I'm not crazy, right?"

"I mean, it is a bit suspect. Two teachers not showing up on day one is odd, for sure." She shrugged. "I don't know if that means something wicked is going on, but I also don't know why Finn has a stick up his butt about it all."

"I don't know either," Mitzi said as her body deflated with a deep sigh. "Let's just get out of here."

Rose nodded as her attention shifted to someone a few feet away. "Hey look, Mitz. Trent is over there."

Mitzi couldn't help but look over at him. He was chatting with the guy standing next to him, but looked over and locked eyes with Mitzi for a moment. She glanced down, her cheeks burning, hating the fact that he caught her looking at him.

"Let's just go, please," she mumbled under her breath as she stood to leave. She reached out her hand to help Rose up, and someone bumped hard into her. She stumbled and turned to see who so rudely pushed her and almost swallowed her tongue, face to face with Trent.

"Hey, watch it!" he snarled at her.

"Sorry! I didn't mean to... Hey, wait a minute!" she said, her annoyance growing. "You bumped into me!"

He looked Mitzi over, with a nasty smirk on his face that sent a rush of confusion down her body.

"Just don't touch me!" he said, and shook his head. "And quit staring at me, too."

He turned and left her standing there, embarrassed, upset, and completely perplexed. He had always been so nice. She even thought that he had a thing for her. But now? Now she wanted to crawl into a deep dark hole and die.

Rose put her head on Mitzi's shoulder as she stood frozen, fighting the urge to cry.

"That made no sense at all, girl," Rose said softly. "Are you alright?"

"I'm fine," she lied. "I never really cared for him much anyway."

"Oh good," Rose said, grabbing Mitzi's hand and leading her to the door. "He smells like cat turds. Never liked him."

"Exactly like cat turds." Mitzi laughed, trying to shake off the hurt she was feeling. "I'm so glad this day is over. I just want to eat and call it a day. It's been a long one, you know."

"Same," Rose said as the two walked slowly through the light rain, toward the pavilion for an early dinner. "I really hope tomorrow is a better day."

Mitzi suddenly stopped walking, jerking Rose, who was still holding her hand, to a quick stop. "What?" Rose asked. "What is it, Mitz?"

"I just got the urge to swing by Nurse Alex's

cabin," she said.

"What are you churning around in that brain of yours now?" Rose said with a smile.

"Oh, you'll see," she said. "Now let's go before your headache gets any worse."

Rose looked confused. "Mitzi, I don't have a head…. oh, right. I got it."

"Good! Now let's go!" Mitzi said as the two took off running.

Chapter Sixteen

"Here, Rose," Nurse Alex said as he handed Rose a little brown pill and a glass of water. "Take that and your headache should go away within the hour."

Rose pretended to take the pill, and took a long pull from the glass. "Thanks, Alex. Sorry to bug you with a boo boo."

"It's no trouble," he said. "You two headed down to dinner?"

Mitzi chimed in. "Yep. Tech was canceled. But I bet you already knew that."

Alex's face turned white and his eyes widened. "What do you mean? Why would you say that?"

"I just assumed that Mr. Bell was sick, too," Mitzi said matter-of-factly. "He never showed up to teach."

"Oh, right…right." Alex went behind his desk and started shuffling through papers. "He is probably sick, too. Haven't had a call to see him yet."

"How is Ms. Walker doing?" Rose asked. "Any updates?"

"No updates yet, girls," he said, still shuffling papers. "I expect she will be as good as new in no time. Now, if you don't mind, I have some paperwork to attend to before dinner."

"Okay, sure," Mitzi said as the two girls turned to leave. "See you tomorrow."

The rain had slowed down to a light mist as the two made their way through the fields, toward the pavilion.

"See," Rose said. "Don't you feel better?"

"Not at all!" said Mitzi. "Now, more than ever, I feel like something is going on. Think about it. Two teachers are supposedly sick and the camp nurse clearly doesn't know anything about it. Don't you think his reaction was a bit strange?"

"You do have a point there," Rose said. "But what do you think is going on?"

"I don't know, Rose," Mitzi said, and stopped walking just short of the food line, so as not to be overheard. "I just have that feeling in my gut. I can't explain it. I just know that something isn't right."

"You're probably just hungry." Rose laughed. "Or tired, or both. Maybe you just need to eat, and then sleep on it."

Mitzi rubbed her face and thought carefully about Rose's advice. She *was* hungry and tired. Maybe her imagination was just running away from her.

"You're right, Rose," Mitzi said. "Let's get some food. Then, hopefully, a good night's sleep will snap me out of it."

"Only one way to find out!" Rose said as she hooked her arm through Mitzi's and the two found their place in the dinner line. "Is that Finn over there, sitting with that Jeremy kid?"

Standing on her tip toes, Mitzi craned her neck and saw Finn sitting with the rude Senior at the back corner table. "That's strange. I guess he's *really* mad at me."

"But he wasn't there on the porch when that guy was a jerk," Rose said. "I'm sure he wouldn't sit with him otherwise."

"Yeah, you're probably right," Mitzi said as she felt her head start to throb. "I'm just gonna head to bed early. I'm not feeling hungry anymore."

Rose shot her a sympathetic look. "Okay, girl, see you tomorrow."

Mitzi walked through the field, the cold mist kissing her face, with her head down. Then, she did something she hadn't done in a very long time. She cried. Today had been horrible. She had gotten herself in trouble, fought with her best friend twice, and then Trent was so heart-crushingly nasty. Topping it all off was the fact that she knew something bad was going down at camp and no one believed her. Not even Rose. Rose was being nice, at least. But Mitzi knew she was on her own, and it felt awful.

Chapter Seventeen

"Mitzi!" a sharp whisper pierced through the darkness. "Mitzi!"

The voice caused Mitzi to stir in her bed, and she startled awake in a heart thumping terror when something suddenly started shaking her.

"What the?" Mitzi frantically looked around the dark room, disoriented from the sudden break from her deep sleep. Her eyes adjusted and found Seph, standing next to her bed with wide eyes.

Seph seemed frantic and whispered, "I'm sorry I scared you. It's just…"

"Noooo," an eerie groan rang out from the far corner of the room.

Mitzi sat up quickly and scanned the dark room, trying to find the source of the cry. "What the heck was that?"

"Stop! No!" another and very different voice cried out, sending Mitzi down her bunk and to her feet.

"That's why I woke you up!" Seph said. "They've been crying and moaning for the last twenty minutes! At first, I thought one girl must be having a bad dream but the cries are from several different…"

"Ahhhhh," a new cry sounded.

"What do we do?" Seph pleaded.

"Is something over there?" Mitzi asked, still groggy. "How in the world would they all be having nightmares at the same time?"

"I have no clue!" Seph said. "Should we wake them up or something?"

Several more cries and groans filled the air as Mitzi racked her brain, trying to come up with an idea. "Do you have a flashlight? Maybe we should take a look around and if we don't see anything, then we could try to wake them up?"

"Yeah, let's try that," Seph said, disappearing and returning a moment later with a large flashlight. "It's coming from over there." Seph pointed the flashlight's beam toward the far back corner of the room, sweeping it from side to side.

"I don't see anything," Mitzi said. "Shine under the beds maybe?"

The two tip-toed around several of the beds, shining the light under each but not finding any reason for the distress. Seph shrugged. Mitzi checked on each of the girls in the area. Nothing seemed out of place other than the fact that Anya's still sleeping face was covered in beads of sweat.

"That's strange," Seph said.

"What?"

"No one is crying anymore," Seph said as she

and Mitzi went back to their bunks. "What the heck was that all about?"

"I have no clue!" Mitzi said as she climbed back into her bunk. "I have never heard of such a thing. I don't think it's possible they would all have a nightmare at the *same* time, and the heaters are all electric, so there's not a gas leak making them all crazy."

"I wonder if it was something they all ate?" Seph said.

"Everyone eats the same food, though, and no one else is crying," whispered Mitzi. "I suppose they all could have had the same snacks from the shack, but I think the bad food theory is a stretch."

"Should we report it?" Seph asked, shrugging her shoulders.

Mitzi wasn't sure what they should do. The crying had passed, and although it was really strange, it seemed to be over with and no real damage had been done.

"Maybe not," she said. "But if it happens again, we definitely should. How about that?"

"Yeah," Seph agreed, and crawled back into her bed. "Sorry I woke you up, but it was so creepy and I didn't know what to do."

"That's okay. I would have done the same thing. Night, Seph."

"Goodnight," Seph said, and rolled over on her side, facing the other way.

Mitzi was wide awake now. She looked down on her watch and saw it was just before four in the morning. Her mind was spinning. She stared up at the ceiling, wondering why those girls would all be crying out in their sleep at the same time. Why did they suddenly stop? She was hoping that her second day at camp would be better, but it wasn't starting out so well.

She spent the next couple of hours tossing and turning until she couldn't take it anymore and got up. A couple other campers were awake now, but most were still sleeping, so Mitzi thought a quick shower might help her feel better. As she gathered her clothes and toiletries, she decided that she would start the day fresh and try to ignore the crying craziness, determined that today would be a good day.

***

But it wasn't a good day at all. Rose never showed up at breakfast, and Finn was sitting with Jeremy again. Mitzi tried to catch his attention but he wouldn't look at her and Mitzi felt like it was on purpose. She ended up eating with a few of the girls from her cabin, but no one made any effort to talk to her. Rose caught up with her on the walk to RIOT class but was grouchy and looked exhausted.

"You missed breakfast," Mitzi said. "Everything alright?"

"I'm fine. Just didn't sleep great," she said.

"I know what you mean," Mitzi said. "In the middle of the night, Seph woke me up cause a bunch of girls were having nightmares and it was so weird. I didn't think…"

"People get nightmares," Rose interrupted. "Man, I wish I had time to get a coffee."

Mitzi was offended by Rose's rude interruption but decided to let it go, in favor of keeping things happy for the day.

"If you want, we can run to the shack after class?" Mitzi offered. "I could use a cup myself."

"Yeah, whatever," Rose said flatly as they scanned into the class to find Ms. Linda sitting behind the teacher's desk, staring down at her tablet.

As soon as the clock struck nine, Linda jumped right into her lesson. Unfortunately, the lesson was on basic secrecy regulations for SHUT members. She talked for an hour about the importance of keeping all SHUT matters completely confidential and the importance of only communicating through SHUT's secured devices. She told story after story about different members of SHUT, and how they screwed up and almost brought the whole organization down. One story in particular caught Mitzi's attention.

"Another member of SHUT was foolish enough to give confidential information to a mimic," Linda said as she glared at Mitzi. "That slip up led to a very dark and powerful weapon ending up in the wrong hands."

Mitzi shrunk down in her chair, hoping no one knew that Linda was talking about her mishap with the mimic over the Covenant Cube. Mitzi knew it wasn't really her fault that the blood vials were in the open, but, apparently, other SHUT members thought that it was.

When the hour was finally done, Mitzi was the first out of her chair and she raced out the door, not making eye contact with anyone along the way.

Rose came out of the class with a scowl on her face and headed straight for Mitzi. "What an awful cow. I can't believe she threw you under the bus like that."

"You think everyone knew she was talking about me?" Mitzi pleaded.

"Duh," Rose said rudely without elaborating at all.

They went to the shack without saying anything else. Mitzi's mood was starting to crumble and she didn't feel like talking anymore.

HAC class was just as miserable. Finn wouldn't even look at Mitzi, and Rose was still grouchy and cold. Mr. Ross seemed like he was still annoyed with her and wouldn't make eye contact either. Mitzi was sleepy and found it hard to focus on his lesson, but tried to look alert and interested so as not to insult him any more than she already had.

After class, Finn stormed out without a word, and Rose informed her that she was having lunch with Seph and that they would, "Catch up later at job time."

So Mitzi ate her second meal alone, looking around the room, completely confused by her current situation. To make matters worse, Rose and Seph were sitting with Finn and Jeremy in the back corner. Mitzi knew why Finn was annoyed with her but couldn't figure out why on earth Rose was acting this way. Why wouldn't she have just asked Mitzi to eat with her and Seph?

It's because she wants to hang with Finn and he won't come near me. Is Rose taking Finn's side? It sure seems like it. UGH! Why is everything falling apart? This was supposed to be a good day.

A sudden fight broke out between two boys in the food line. A garbage bin went flying through the air and a piece of a half-chewed sandwich landed on Mitzi's tray with a squishy thud. "I guess I'm done with lunch," Mitzi said out loud to herself as she stood and walked around the crowd of fight-watchers to dump her tray. At least her next class was Pharma. No Finn or Rose in there. Thank God.

Pharma was definitely the highlight of the day. Ms. Stukes was in a chipper mood and Mitzi found her cheerful demeanor contagious. The class was interesting, too. They spent the hour learning about the twelve uses of garnet stone, and Mitzi was completely lost in the learning and was grateful for the hour-long escape from the day's reality.

During Weapons and Survival, Mitzi didn't even bother trying to find Finn, and tried her best to ignore him when she saw him with a group of boys in the field. Instructor Dodge wasn't anywhere to be seen, so the campers just huddled in groups, waiting on some direction.

Mitzi stood next to Jayde and Charlie, but they didn't engage her at all, leaving her feeling as lonely as ever. It was cold and damp and a chill ran through Mitzi and she wasn't sure if it was from the weather or the growing betrayal she was feeling. Out of the corner of her eye, she noticed Linda squishing her way through the field and toward them and realized what Dodge's absence must have meant…another teacher down.

Linda stopped just short of the students and

cleared her throat. She stood still, expressionless, and waited for the conversations to die out, which took only moments.

"It seems as though Instructor Dodge is down with illness now, too. You will be on free time today. Tomorrow, I have asked one of our new campers, Millie Von Barron, to teach the class the basics of archery training. She is an expert in her field, and you will extend to her the same respect as any other professor. That is all."

She turned and squished away, and the campers' chatter instantly resumed. "You can't tell me that," Mitzi turned to Finn, and finding Charlie instead, she sadly remembered he wasn't there and mumbled to herself, "this is not suspicious."

"What?" Charlie asked with a confused look on her face.

"Oh, sorry," Mitzi said. "I was just saying it's

weird that so many teachers are sick."

"Yeah," Charlie said. "It's crazy that so many teachers are sick and not a single camper is. Hope it stays that way. I hate getting sick."

"Charlie, you're a genius!" Mitzi said as she took off running. She had almost two hours before jobs, and she was gonna use them to find some answers. Even if that meant doing it all alone.

Chapter Eighteen

Mitzi stepped into the health cabin, out of breath from running, and waved hello to Alex, who was sitting behind his desk.

"Well, you're a bit early for jobs, Mitzi," he said with a smile. "To what do I owe this pleasure?"

"I need your help," Mitzi said.

His smile faded and he motioned to a chair for her to sit down. "What can I do for you?"

"I think that something bad is going on at camp, and you are the only one who may be able to help me figure things out," Mitzi said in one long breath, as she watched his reaction very carefully.

"Why do you think something bad is going on?"

"Because another teacher is sick, and correct

me if I'm wrong, but you don't know anything about it."

"What makes you think I don't know anything about…"

"Oh, come on," Mitzi interrupted. "You aren't a very good actor, and you obviously didn't know about Ms. Walker or Mr. Bell and…"

"Okay, okay, okay!" he said, throwing his hands up in the air. "I just didn't want you guys to think I was out of the loop. But, honestly, people get sick all the time and don't necessarily seek out treatment, you know?"

"So you pretended to know they were sick so…?"

"So you and your friends wouldn't think I was lame. Right."

Mitzi frowned, unsure if she believed him.

"You gotta understand. None of the adults

here are particularly fond of me, so they keep me in the dark on most things around here."

"Why would you say they aren't fond of you?"

"Because they aren't!" He chuckled. "I haven't *exactly* been shy about how much I dislike being stuck here, and that hasn't won me any friends. I am sorry that I misled you, though. I should have just been honest."

Mitzi nodded, still unsure of his explanation. "So you don't know if those teachers are really sick or not then, do you?"

"I have no idea," he said. "But, Mitzi, what makes you think they aren't sick? Why fake an illness?"

"That's the part that I can't quite figure out. All I know is that no one has actually *seen* anyone sick. Linda just keeps *telling* us that. That's why I came to you for help."

"What could I possibly do?" he said. "I have already told you I don't have any friends here."

"I thought you could stop by the sick teachers' rooms to check on them."

"What are you expecting me to find, though?" he said, scratching his head in confusion.

"I don't know," Mitzi said honestly. "But it seems like a good place to start."

Alex leaned back in his chair and rubbed his face. "I think I have an even better idea." He reached into his desk drawer and pulled out a tablet. Mitzi tried to see the screen as he pressed different spots and navigated through several screens but couldn't quite make anything out.

"Well, isn't that crazy," he said as he handed Mitzi the tablet. "I think you actually may be onto something."

Mitzi looked at what appeared to be an aerial

view of the entire camp. There were tiny little red and blue dots moving all over the screen.

"What are all of the dots?" Mitzi asked.

"The red are students and the blue are staff," he said. "There are trackers in everyone's watches."

"Wow," Mitzi said. "I guess they do have some serious security around here."

"You have no idea!" he said. "The scan system is only the tip of the iceberg."

"Okay, so how do we know who is who on here?"

"We don't," he said. "At least, I don't have access to that info."

"So then what are we looking for on here? I'm confused."

"I thought if three teachers are in fact sick, they would be in their bed. Or at least in their apartment. But if you look at the staff building, it's empty."

Mitzi looked at the building and was surprised to find not a single blue dot. "That leaves a big question then. Where the heck are they?"

"Exactly! You know when you first came in and told me your concern, I thought you were just being paranoid. But I see now, you are actually onto something. Who else have you told about this?"

Mitzi handed him back the tablet, carefully deciding how she should answer. "No one. I thought maybe I was being paranoid, too, and I didn't want everyone to think I was crazy. Where would the teachers go, though? I haven't heard any boats or planes. They couldn't have just disappeared."

"That gives me an idea!" Alex leaned over his tablet again. "I think they must have disappeared."

"What do you mean? Show me," Mitzi said, reaching out for the tablet.

"I have overlaid our infrared heat signature filter on top of the map with the dots. There is no sign of anyone other than where all the dots are."

"Oh! I think I get it. Their body heat would show up as a red spot on here, right?"

Alex nodded.

"So those three teachers really are missing," Mitzi said flatly.

"Or dead," he said as Mitzi felt a horrified expression take over her face. "I just mean that is the only way a body wouldn't give off some kind of heat."

"Well, in that case," Mitzi said softly, "I hope they are only missing."

Mitzi sat quietly considering whether or not to tell Alex about her overheard conversation in the woods but decided against it.

"What do we do now?" Mitzi asked.

"I'm going to talk to Linda. She must know what's going on," he said and stood.

"Linda?" Mitzi was surprised he named her of all people. "What if she's in on it?"

"Oh, I think she must know that they are missing and not sick, but she loves this camp more than life itself. I think she can be trusted."

"What should I do?" she asked.

"Sit tight," he said. "Your friends should be here for jobs in less than an hour. I should be back before then."

"Okay. I'll wait here," she said, relieved to have some quiet time to process the new information.

"And, Mitzi," Alex said as he opened the door, "I wouldn't talk about this with anyone. We don't know who can be trusted. Be back soon."

"Good luck," Mitzi said as the door closed,

leaving her alone with her thoughts.

Chapter Nineteen

Mitzi jumped when the door opened forty-five minutes later, expecting Alex with news, but was slightly bummed by the sight of Rose and Finn instead.

The air in the room seemed to thicken, as Rose sat down at the opposite end of the couch and Finn sat in the chair by the desk. No one said a word, and the three sat for several minutes in awkward silence until Mitzi couldn't take it anymore.

"Rose?" she said softly. "Did I do something to make you mad at me? What's with the silent treatment all of a sudden?

Rose turned to her and dramatically rolled her eyes. "No. I just needed a break from you. You make a big deal out of everything and sometimes it gets old."

Ouch. Mitzi flinched at her words and felt the sudden urge to defend herself. "No I don't. Trouble just has a way of finding me," she grumbled.

Finn laughed, adding to Mitzi's anger. "What's funny here, Finn? Every time I have had my suspicions, they turned out to be right. Why are you being so nasty to me?" Emotion cracked through her voice and she could feel tears building in her eyes, which she tried to blink away. Her own emotion made her angry. She wasn't sad, she was angry and hurt, and didn't want Finn or Rose to see her looking weak.

"Whatever," Finn said. "So when exactly is camp supposed to crumble around us? Seems fine to me."

"Fine?" Mitzi shook her head, trying to find the right words to say to set them both straight.

"Nothing is fine! Three teachers have some mysterious illness, after I overhear a strange and threatening conversation in the middle of the night, not to mention the fact that most of the campers are acting like a dark cloud is hanging over them. Especially the both of you! We have been friends our entire lives and neither one of you has ever been so nasty ever before! I haven't even told you about last night. About the cries and nightmares throughout my cabin. Nothing is fine!

"Nightmares?" Rose said softly. "What about the nightmares?"

"I tried to tell you earlier and you wouldn't listen. Seph woke me up in the middle of the night because several girls were crying and calling out in their sleep. We looked around, but couldn't find anything. They just seemed to be having a nightmare, all at the same time."

"The last two nights, I've been having nightmares," Rose said softly. "I've never had them, so I didn't know what to think, but, Mitzi, it's been absolutely terrifying." A single tear ran down Rose's cheek.

Mitzi felt terrible for her friend, having never seen her cry before. Rose wasn't a crier. But she also felt a rush of relief as if the nightmares explained Rose's uncharacteristic behaviors.

"Do you remember what the dreams were about?" Mitzi asked.

"I do." Finn's voice cut through Mitzi like a hot knife through butter. "Two nights in a row I've had the same dream. I'm in a pit and it's so dark and can't even see my hands in front of my face. Something starts digging into me, burning my guts, and I try to run but I can't. Then it starts pushing me. I fall and get back up and get pushed again. I scream for help but I just keep getting pushed down again and again and again by something I can't see."

"Finn," Mitzi said, "that's absolutely horrible. Why didn't you just tell us?"

He shrugged. "I don't know. I feel so angry. So sad and off. I don't mean to be so horrible to you. I just can't seem to help myself."

"Same," Rose said as she closed her eyes. "My dreams are similar. Except I'm running in mine, and just when I think I've outrun it, it grabs my face and I run in a new direction. Frantically. Over and over and over again."

"Clearly, something is attacking the campers with something that causes nightmares," Mitzi said matter-of-factly. "But what on earth would cause everyone to have the same nightmare? Actually, it's not everyone. Why some kids and not others? This is definitely the strangest thing I have ever heard."

"Some kind of mass hysteria?" Rose asked.

"Mind control?" Finn said. "I wouldn't put that past Linda. She seems a bit off."

Mitzi looked at the door. Alex should have been back by now. "Speaking of Linda, I think it's time I fill you in on the current situation, that is, assuming we are somewhat back to normal here."

"I'm sorry, Mitzi," Rose said. "I didn't know I was so troubled about the nightmares. I have been horrible to you."

"Me too," Finn said. "Sorry."

"It's all over with, as far as I'm concerned," Mitzi said firmly. "You both get a pass. I think you are being attacked in your sleep. That would give anyone a pass. Now, let me fill you in on the new developments. I'll start with why Alex isn't here."

Chapter Twenty

"He's been gone for almost two hours now, you guys," Mitzi said. "Something's not right. I can feel it."

"But what should we do?" Rose asked. "We can't just go for help. We don't know who we can trust."

"I think we should go to Linda," Finn said.

"Are you crazy, Finn?" Rose whined. "She could be the reason Alex is missing, and then she will know we are onto her! God only knows what she would do to us?"

"Not if we play dumb, though," Mitzi said. "Maybe we just go and say that Nurse Alex never showed up for jobs. Tell her that we weren't sure if maybe he was sick, too, and we thought we should let her know."

"I guess that makes sense," Rose said slowly. "But she will just lie to us, so what good will it do?"

"I don't know," admitted Mitzi, "but at least we could see how she reacts. Maybe she will accidentally give up some information. I don't know but it's all I got!"

"More than I've got, so we might as well give it a try, I guess," Rose relented.

The three headed out into the rain and took off in a run toward the staff house. A sign on the door read, **Students must ring the bell**, and Mitzi let out a sigh and mumbled, "Here goes nothing," before pressing the little black button by the door.

"Who is it, and how can I help you?" Linda's voice crackled from a speaker above the door.

"It's Mitzi, Rose, and Finn," Mitzi said loudly. "We are here because Nurse Alex never showed up for jobs and we thought we should report it to you."

The three waited several moments for a response. "He's most likely down with the same bug as the other teachers." Her voice sounded hurried, shaky, and unsure. "Thank you for reporting this. I will go and check on him. You may be on free time now."

The three turned away and slowly walked through the rain back toward the health cabin.

"Well, that was a giant waste of time," Finn grumbled.

"Maybe not," Mitzi said. "I don't think Alex ever made it to see her."

"What makes you think that?" Rose said with a very confused look on her face.

"I just think if Alex had been there, she would have been expecting us to show up and she sounded surprised to me. She knows that jobs are everyday at the same time. Don't you think she would have showed up at the health cabin to cover her tracks if she was behind his disappearance?"

"Good point," Finn said. "But then why is she keeping with the whole 'teachers are sick' thing? She has to know they are missing."

"Think about it," Mitzi said, shrugging her shoulders. "If you were her, would you tell the kids that the teachers are missing? Or would you come up with a lie while trying to figure it out and keep everyone from panicking?"

"Makes sense, I guess," said Finn. "But how many people have to vanish before she calls for help, or closes camp and sends us all home?"

"I'm sure that Linda is asking herself that same question right now," Mitzi said. "What are we gonna do next, guys? Any ideas?"

"How about we head to the shack and get out

of this rain? I'm freezing!" Rose suggested.

Finn nodded his agreement. "Hot cocoa sounds pretty darn good right about now."

"Then maybe after that we could head to the pavilion and come up with a plan?" Mitzi asked. "At least *try* to come up with one?"

"Sure," Finn said.

"We can try," Rose added.

Just then, Finn took off running. "Last one there is a crusty turd!" he yelled over his shoulder.

Rose took off after him, squealing. "*Really*, Finny? How old are you?"

Mitzi smiled for the first time all day. Instead of running after them, she just walked, watching them through the rain, happy to have her friends back. It had been so hard, trying to figure out any of this mystery without them by her side. And she had a feeling that things were about to get messy.

Chapter Twenty-One

"Correct me if I'm wrong here, but so far, we have to figure out where the missing teachers went," Finn said while messaging his temples with his forefinger and thumb. "Plus, we need to see if we can figure out who this 'John' guy is, *and* try to find the cause for all of the nightmares?"

"That sounds like a piece of cake," Rose said sarcastically.

"In the morning," Mitzi said, "I'll ask Ms. Stukes about the name John. She's worked here forever, so if anyone would know, it would be her."

"I can try to sniff around at the marina," Finn said. "I know a boy who has jobs down there. Maybe he's seen boats coming in and out that we don't know about?"

"I think I know what I can do," Rose mumbled. "I think I am gonna stay awake to see if I can find anything triggering the nightmares in my cabin."

"Sure you are up for it?" Mitzi asked, concerned for her friend.

Rose gave her a warm smile. "I don't really want to go to sleep anyway, so yeah, I'll be fine."

"Well, I guess that's a good place to start," Mitzi said as Finn's face fell into a scowl. "What is it, Finn?"

"I hate to say it," he said, "but if the teachers are still on this island, there's a good chance they're dead. Maybe we should grid out the forest and search for bodies?"

Mitzi groaned. "I don't want to admit it, but you're right. We can start after dinner. That will give us a few hours before it gets dark."

Their watches suddenly buzzed, reminding them that Tech started in ten minutes, and Rose shook her head. "I don't feel like sitting through another boring Linda lecture right now, ugh."

"Maybe we will get lucky and *she* will disappear," Finn said with a very mischievous grin on his face.

Rose let out a short giggle, but recovered herself quickly. "Boy, you are not right in the head!"

"Whatever," he said defensively. "You were both thinking it."

"Maybe for a split second," Mitzi admitted with a chuckle as she stood up from the table. "Let's go to Tech and get this over with."

"That's the spirit," Finn said as he and Rose got up to leave.

They stepped back into the rain and Rose let out a groan. "Will it ever stop raining?" she whined.

"I hope so," Mitzi said. "At least in time for our grid search tonight."

"Oh, come on, Mitzi," Finn said in a sarcastic, overly cheerful voice. "Who doesn't like to look for dead bodies in a dark and rainy forest? I've been looking forward to this for so long. When I read about it in the camp brochure, I just knew I had to come here."

Mitzi laughed. "Finn, honestly…"

"Last one there is a rotting corpse!" Finn yelled as he took off running again.

"Not this time!" Rose shouted as she took off after him. Only this time, Mitzi was hot on her heels and didn't even care about the rain.

***

Tech class was cut short again, leaving the three with another possible clue to sort out. Linda stood under the giant screen and, looking completely worn out, let the students know that the evening lesson, which was supposed to be on AIDA, SHUT's Artificial Intelligence Database Analyst, was cancelled until further notice.

"The entire island's communication system is down and we are working very hard to fix the issue as soon as possible. Please continue to scan in and out as that system is on a separate network."

As per usual, Linda did not elaborate and quickly left the building.

"Well, that is actually good news," Mitzi said to Finn and Rose as the other campers noisily filed out of the building.

"How do you figure?" Rose asked.

"If the coms are down," Mitzi said, "then parents won't be able to contact the camp. Surely someone will find it suspicious and send help."

"You are forgetting about the camp's two-week rule, Mitzi," Finn grumbled.

"Two-week rule?" Mitzi was confused.

"Yep. Parents are advised to not reach out to campers during the first two weeks at camp, to give the kids time to adjust to their new environment. My dad was told that he would be contacted by me, as soon as the two-weeks were over."

Mitzi groaned. "That's outrageous. What if there is an emergency back home?"

"My dad was given a phone number in case of an emergency, but I don't know anything else about it," Finn said.

Mitzi looked slowly from Finn to Rose, trying to think of a way to send for help, but couldn't come up with one. "I guess we *are* on our own."

"You guys," Rose said sounding alarmed, "what do we even do if we find the missing teachers? You know, in the woods. It's not like we can call the cops. What then?"

Rose had a point. Mitzi pictured herself in the woods, walking up on a pile of teacher bodies, and shuddered. "I'm really hoping that's a question we will never have to answer, but I don't know."

"Let's not get ahead of ourselves," Finn said calmly. "I think it's more likely that they left the island somehow. We have time before dinner. I'm going to the marina to see if I can find out anything. I'll meet up with you guys at dinner, and we will go from there.

Finn left, leaving Mitzi and Rose alone in the big room. Mitzi stood and started pacing, as Rose sat and watched her. With her mind buzzing with questions, she started mumbling to herself. "Why *these* teachers in particular? Are they just a part of the scheme? If they *did* leave the island, where would they go? If they were taken, *who* would have taken them?

As far as that overheard conversation during midnight mayhem, what is going to happen come Friday night?"

She stopped pacing and took a look around the room, noticing a small plaque on the wall near the corner that she hadn't noticed before. Walking up to it, she called out to Rose, "I just found a possible clue. It's a Plaque of the Fallen Heroes of SHUT, and it has about sixty or so names on it. There might me something important here."

But as Rose came over to look, Mitzi scanned the names and was disappointed when nothing of interest jumped out at her.

"Nothing is grabbing my attention," Rose said as she shrugged at Mitzi.

"Me neither," Mitzi said softly. "I was hoping for a break, but I guess not. What should we do now? Any ideas?"

"Maybe we should go look through Alex's stuff and see if he knew more than he was letting on?"

"I guess it's worth a try, but what about our watches?" asked Mitzi. "If someone pulls up the map and sees us in there, what would we say?"

"We just tell them that I lost my retainer, and we are retracing our steps to see if we left it somewhere," Rose said matter-of-factly.

Mitzi smiled. "I like it. Especially since you haven't had a retainer sense the fifth grade."

Rose giggled. "What are we waiting for? Let's go."

It was a quick walk to the health cabin, and a handwritten sign was hanging from the door that read, **Closed for the night, report to staff cabin for an emergency**.

Mitzi was shocked when they found the door

unlocked. "Let's move quickly. I have a bad feeling about this."

"Okay," Rose said, and nodded. "How about I check around the room, while you search his desk?"

Mitzi nodded and went behind the large wood desk but didn't see anything that looked odd or out of place. She sat down in the chair and started opening the drawers. Finding the first two filled with the usual desk stuff, Mitzi sighed in frustration as she pulled open the larger bottom drawer, finding it a filing cabinet. Each of the folder tabs had a camper's name on it and were in alphabetical order. She thumbed through the files quickly, and was tempted to stop at her own folder, but kept going for the sake of time. When she got to the last file, she could tell there was something behind it, so she pulled the folders to the front of the drawer as best as she could and reached in the deep drawer and pulled out an old-looking, small, black book.

"Whatcha got there?" Rose asked as she came around the desk to join Mitzi.

"Not sure yet," Mitzi said, turning the book around in her hands before carefully opening it.

Rose read the title page over Mitzi's shoulder, "The Poems of Emily Dickenson. Okay. A book of poetry. Meh."

"But why hide it way in the back of the drawer?" Mitzi said, flipping carefully through the old pages, coming to an abrupt stop when she landed on photo of a young woman, used as a bookmark. "She's very pretty. Wonder who she is."

"Probably an old girlfriend," Rose said, and then pointed down at the book. "That poem is circled. What are the chances we'd find another clue in a book? Read it and let's see."

"Okay," Mitzi said as she brought the little

book closer to her face.

> "If I could stop one heart from breaking,
> I shall not live in vain;
> If I can ease one life the aching,
> Or cool one pain,
> Or help one fainting robin
> Unto his nest again,
> I shall not live in vain."

Mitzi wordlessly tucked the photo back into the book and returned it to the back of the drawer. "I don't really understand poetry, but that one made me sad."

"Same," Rose said. "I don't think there is anything here, Mitzi. We should just get out of here."

"I think you're right," she agreed. But as they opened the door to leave, a very angry-looking Linda was glaring down at them. She stepped toward them, forcing them back into the cabin and yelled, "Sit down, you two!"

Mitzi glanced over at Rose, who was looking as terrified as Mitzi was feeling. She could feel her heart pounding in her ears as she sat next to Rose on the couch. Linda stood facing them both, hands on her hips, chest heaving.

"You both have some serious explaining to do so one of you needs to start talking right now!" Linda yelled.

"I think you have the wrong idea, ma'am," Rose said bravely. "I lost my retainer and Mitzi and I were just retracing our steps to see if I left it here."

Mitzi nodded to corroborate Rose's story.

Linda bit the inside of her cheek like she was considering whether or not to believe the excuse. "You never scanned in," she said suspiciously. "If you were just here looking for your retainer, why didn't you scan in?"

"We must have forgot!" Mitzi said. "We were so surprised to find the door unlocked that scanning in must have slipped our minds. We are very sorry."

Linda didn't say a word but dropped her hands down to her side and started slowly pacing the small room. Mitzi, watching her pace, had a sudden and potentially reckless idea.

"You don't know where he is, do you?" she said bravely as both females turned and shot her looks of fear and confusion.

"What are you doing?" Rose whispered before slapping her hand to her forehead.

"Excuse me?" Linda hissed and took a step toward them. "What on earth would make you say such a thing?"

"Because I happen to think that all of the sick

teachers are missing and you might even have something to do with it." Mitzi thought that her heart might actually explode. She couldn't believe she was confronting Linda and desperately hoped she wouldn't live to regret it.

"That's absolutely absurd!" Linda snapped.

"Which part?" Mitzi pushed. "That they have disappeared? Or that you had something to do with it?"

"I had nothing to do with it!" she yelled, seeming to unravel before their eyes. "I mean both. I mean...I need to sit down."

She turned around the chair by the desk, to face the couch, and sat down. After a minute of deep breathing with her eyes closed, she cleared her throat.

"Why do you think the teachers are missing?" she asked.

"Because Nurse Alex showed me the watch

tracking map, and all their rooms are empty. They're not there," Mitzi said, unflinching.

"And why would he show you that?" Linda asked.

"Because it was strange that three teachers had fallen ill with a mysterious illness, but no campers had reported any sickness. I think he showed me the map to settle my doubts. But he seemed pretty shocked himself to see that the teachers weren't there."

"When did this happen?" Linda asked. "Why didn't he just come to me?"

"Right before jobs today," Mitzi said. "He did go to you, right away."

"Yeah, and he never came back," Rose added. "Kind of makes you the prime suspect."

"If he had come to me," Linda said, "I would agree with you about that. But, as it is, he never came to see me."

"How do we know you are telling us the truth?" Mitzi asked.

"Because I can prove it with the same tracker map," she said, pulling a mini tablet from her back pocket and tapping on the screen several times. "Okay, here. I've scrubbed back to when I see him leaving the health cabin…. he's walking across the field… There! His signal just stops moving. Look for yourself."

She scrubbed the video back and handed the device to Rose.

"Do you think he took off his watch and dropped it in the field, maybe to leave us a clue?" Mitzi asked while watching the map carefully.

"Maybe," Linda said. "We will go out and see in a minute but first I think we need to talk."

Mitzi handed Linda back her device. "We're listening."

"Normally, I would never bring campers in on such an important matter, but I don't know what adults here I can trust anymore. I don't know what to do. I have scoured the surveillance videos and have found nothing. Last night, I came to the conclusion that it was time to call for back up, only to find that we are completely cut off. I don't want to create a panic at camp, but I would die if anything started happening to the kids." A single tear ran down her face.

"Couldn't someone take a boat to go get help?" Rose asked softly.

"I thought of that," Linda said, "But it would be a full day's journey, and Instructor Dodge is the only one trained enough for that kind of trip."

"What about a plane?" Mitzi asked. "Are we expecting one anytime soon?"

Her face lit up. "Mitzi! You are a genius! We

have a supply run scheduled for Friday! We just have to last a couple more days. But, oh, that seems like a long way off in this situation."

"It's a start, at least," Rose said. "In the meantime, maybe we can figure out how to fix the coms, or better yet, solve the case."

Linda stood up quickly. "I expect regular reports from the two of you. Now let's go and see if there is a watch laying somewhere in the field. Then you both can head out for dinner."

"Sounds good," Mitzi said as she and Rose followed Linda out of the cabin, and onto the field. Linda using her tablet to watch the three of them inch closer and closer to the still dot on the screen.

"There it is," Rose pointed, and Linda bent down and snatched the very wet watch off the ground before stuffing in into her pocket.

"Alright, girls," she said. "Go and eat. Don't

discuss this with anyone. We will touch base tomorrow, but let me know if you find out anything else before then.

She huffed away toward the staff cabin, leaving Mitzi and Rose standing in the field.

"Why didn't you tell her about the nightmares?" Rose asked. "Or about the conversation you overheard? Seems like it could all be pretty useful information."

"Because, Rose," Mitzi said in just over a whisper, "I still don't think that we can trust her. There's something she's not telling us. I can just feel it."

Chapter Twenty-Two

Finn took a bite of his burger and started talking with his mouth full. "I'm telling you guys, there's no way a boat has left those docks in the last few days. Security is tight! Log books, video surveillance, whole nine yards!"

A small bit of mush flew out of his mouth and landed on Rose's elbow. "Gross, Finny! Don't talk with food in your mouth." she whined. "They must be here someplace then. If they are still alive, where could they be hiding without leaving a heat signature on the thermal cam?"

"That's a good question," Finn said through another bite of his burger in his mouth. "Maybe underground? Or a building with a metal roof?"

"If they were in any building, we would see

their dot on the tracker screen, though," Mitzi said.

"Not if their watches have been smashed," Finn said, shrugging. "I think we should look in the forest first. For bodies, or any sign of a cave… or dug up hole."

"A cave!" Rose said and shuddered. "Haven't thought about that possibility. Reminds me of that awful werewolf den we were in last year."

"Don't remind me," Mitzi groaned. "The last thing we need around here are a bunch of werewolves."

***

Other than several mosquito bites, the three-hour search through the woods was completely uneventful. Tired, wet, and cold, the three set off to their cabins for some much-needed rest, with plans to pick up their search the next day. Mitzi was exhausted. The moment her head hit the pillow, she fell into a very deep and dreamless sleep.

In the morning, a very worn looking out Rose was waiting for her outside. Her hair was a mess and her eyes bloodshot, and Mitzi could tell she didn't sleep much at all.

"Looks like you had a rough night," Mitzi said. "Please tell me it was worth it. Did you learn anything? Any more nightmares?"

Rose shook her head. "I forced myself to stay awake all night. Other than one girl talking in her sleep, all was totally quiet."

"That's too bad. I mean, that's good. I mean…"

"I know what you mean," Rose interrupted. "Maybe the whole nightmare thing was just an odd phenomenon, you know?"

"Let's hope so," Mitzi said. "I'm gonna talk to Ms. Stukes today and see if she has any idea who John is. Hopefully, she will know something."

"You should ask her about Alex, too," Rose suggested. "Maybe she would know who the girl in the picture might be."

"Good idea," Mitzi said as she started to yawn. "Now I just need to figure out how I'm going to ask her."

"You'll think of something," Rose said. "Let's grab some breakfast before all the good stuff's gone. Maybe Finn had a more eventful night than we did."

But Finn's night had been just as quiet as everyone else's. "So, I think that we should use today's free time to check the woods behind the senior house. We haven't looked there yet." He stuffed an entire strip of bacon into his mouth.

"Looked for what?" Seph said, approaching the table with Jeremy, surprising all three of them. "What are you three up to?"

"Nothing that would interest you," Rose said. "Just a lost journal."

Seph and Jeremy sat down next to Finn, and Jeremy leaned in and whispered, "I don't buy that. Why would it be behind the Senior house? You three are up to something."

"Come on," Seph whined. "Let us in on it."

"There's nothing to let you in on," Mitzi lied as she turned to Jeremy. "Besides. I don't even know you other than the fact that you were rude to me the day we got here."

Jeremy's face turned very red and he leaned back and ran a hand through his hair. "I'm sorry I was a jerk. I shouldn't have been. It's just…it's just…"

"Your dad cost his dad the promotion he wanted, then had his family relocated to a swamp," Finn explained. "I explained to him that you are not the one he should be mad at, and then he thought about it and came to the same conclusion."

"My dad?" Mitzi was surprised and a bit embarrassed. "How did my dad mess up your father's promotion?"

"It doesn't really matter," he said. "Finn was right. It doesn't have anything to do with you. Sorry that I was a jerk."

Mitzi looked him over carefully. She was willing to accept his apology and move on, but she wasn't ready to trust him yet. "It's water under the bridge."

Seph playfully poked Finn on the shoulder. "Then why don't you tell us what is really going on with you three? We see you whispering and saw you head into the woods last night."

Mitzi stood up and grabbed Rose by the elbow, pulling her into standing position. "It really is nothing. But we gotta go. Don't want to be late for RIOT!" On their way out, Mitzi shot Finn a look that said, *Don't you dare tell them anything.*

"Yes. I better be off to Pharma myself," Mitzi heard Finn say as she dragged the sleepy Rose out of the pavilion and toward RIOT.

Mitzi tried hard to concentrate on Linda's lesson on SHUT's chain of command, but her mind kept drifting to the possible questions she should ask Ms. Stukes. Before she knew it, people were getting up around her. Apparently, class had ended without her noticing.

"Mitzi," Linda said from the desk at the front of the room. "You and Rose hang back for a minute. I want to talk."

"Yes ma'am," Mitzi said, feeling a heat building in her gut.

When the last of the campers scanned out of

the room, Linda looked up from her paperwork and straight at Mitzi. "Anything new?" she asked. "I know you searched the woods last night. Did you find anything?"

Mitzi glanced over at Rose to see if she was gonna answer, but saw her staring blankly forward. "No ma'am. It was a dead end."

"That's too bad," she said. "I was hoping that something would have turned up. Do you have any other ideas?"

"Not really," Mitzi admitted. "We are gonna keep looking, though."

Linda nodded quietly. "Please let me know as soon as you find anything at all. We need to find those teachers. I'm so worried they are in danger."

"What if a camper is behind all of this?" Rose said. "Any idea who might have a grudge against Camp STASH?"

"I've been thinking about that a lot, actually," Linda said, eyes filling with tears. "I really don't know anyone who would be capable of kidnapping several teachers."

A single tear rolled down her cheek. Mitzi shifted uncomfortably in her seat, realizing that Linda really *did* care about the camp and *could* be trusted. Now seemed the perfect time to tell Linda the rest of what they know, but she was nervous about admitting the rule breaking that led to their discovery.

"Ms. Linda," Mitzi said sheepishly. "There is something we haven't told you yet."

Linda dragged her arm across her cheek to wipe away her tear. "What is it?"

"The first night, during midnight mayhem, I snuck out of my cabin." She paused, waiting for Linda to react to her admonition, but she just sat there, stone-faced. "I stumbled upon a secret conversation, between two men in the forest."

"What did you hear? Do you know who they were?" she blurted.

"I don't know who they were but I did hear the name John," she said. "John sounded nervous and they were arguing, but the other guy told him not to worry because they would be gone before the real trouble began on Friday. That's all we could hear."

Linda sat back in her chair and visibly deflated. "Why didn't you tell me that yesterday?" she asked. "Who else knows about this? Was it just the two of you?"

"Rose wasn't there. It was my friend Seph, but she thinks they were just a couple of seniors planning some kind of prank. She hasn't put anything else together." Mitzi squirmed in her chair again. "I didn't tell you yesterday because I honestly didn't know if you could be trusted…thought maybe you were in on the whole thing."

"What changed?" Linda said, looking Mitzi straight in the eyes. "Why do you trust me now?"

"A few reasons, really," Mitzi said. "First, you showed up today. I think you may have gone into hiding if you were involved, knowing we were onto you. Secondly, you seem genuinely upset with all that is happening. And, lastly, they were men's voices in the woods and I think that they are the ones responsible for the missing teachers. I feel it in my gut and my gut never lies."

"It's true," Rose says. "Her gut never lies. It's a gift."

"The problem is that I don't know anyone named John," Linda said. "I know every teacher, cook, cleaner, groundskeeper, security member, and camper, and can't think of a single John."

"Maybe they've given each other code

names," Rose suggested with a shrug.

"Perhaps," Linda said.

Mitzi was struck with a sudden thought. "Could anyone have snuck onto the covers plane? It was the right after the cover kids arrived."

"I don't think so," Linda said. "The security on the airplanes is ridiculously tight. I don't think even a mouse would be able to sneak through."

"So what do we do?" Mitzi asked. "The clock is ticking."

Linda looked at Rose and then back to Mitzi. "I'll see if I can figure out if there is a John here that I'm not remembering. But with communications down, we will have to wait until delivery day to talk to the pilot."

"The pilot!" Rose shrieked.

"What about him?" Linda asked.

"I bet it's him. Seems kind of fishy that he's

flying in supplies the night that 'real trouble' is supposed to go down," Rose said, drawing finger quotes in the air as she spoke.

"No; it wouldn't be him," Linda said with an air of certainty. "I've known Captain Frank for over fifteen years. He's such a good guy. I know it can't be him."

Linda sat back and started strumming her fingernails across the desk. "But I will look into it. Just in case."

"What about us?" Mitzi said. "What would you like us to do?"

"The best thing you can do is to just keep looking," said Linda. "For clues, for my teachers, for anything. If you find anything, please come find me. Now you two better scram. You're late for your next classes. If you get asked, just say you were with me."

Mitzi and Rose stood to leave but another

question came to Mitzi. "What do we do during jobs? Nurse Alex is missing, so what are we supposed to do?"

"Scan into the health cabin, for now," Linda said. "If any first aid calls come in, you can handle them."

"Ugh," Rose groaned.

"But," Linda added, "if you need to go anywhere, searching or investigating any leads, leave your watches behind, so it looks like you are still there if the wrong person is watching the maps."

"Good thinking," Mitzi said as they turned toward the door.

"And girls," Linda yelled, turning them around to face her again, "please be careful out there."

Chapter Twenty-Three

Mr. Ross didn't seem to notice or care when they arrived late to HAC. The class was boring, and Mitzi was glad she only had to sit through about twenty minutes of it. During lunch, they filled Finn in on the conversation with Linda before going their separate ways for their next classes, agreeing to meet up at free time, before jobs.

Pharma class was as engaging as ever. Ms. Stukes gave an exciting lecture on different insects, and their use as medicines and poison. Despite the interesting lesson, Mitzi could not focus much. Now that Linda was looking into the 'who is John' question, Mitzi spent most of Pharma class, trying to come up with some questions to ask Ms. Stukes about Alex. As the students filed out of the room, she sat behind, waiting for her teacher to notice her still sitting there.

Focused on her tablet, Ms. Stukes didn't move for several moments so Mitzi cleared her throat.

"Oh my!" Ms. Stukes exclaimed. "I'm sorry, dear. I didn't realize you were still here. Is there something I can help you with?"

Here goes nothing, Mitzi thought to herself as she took a deep breath. "I was thinking about doing something nice for Nurse Alex and thought you might have some ideas. You see, he's been so nice to me and my friends, and now he has fallen sick and we want to do something nice for him, to make him feel better."

She cringed inside, now hearing out loud how stupid her plan sounded, and was completely shocked when Ms. Stukes seemed to buy it.

"Oh, that's so sweet, dear," she said. "He is

such a nice fellow. I didn't know that he's sick, too. Poor guy. He has the worst luck."

"What do you mean?" Mitzi asked, trying her best to sound sweet and innocent.

"Oh, I probably shouldn't tell you this, dear, but he lost his young girlfriend last year. She was out on a SHUT mission and took a nasty fall. Didn't make it. I can't imagine how hard it all must be for him."

"Wow," Mitzi said, her head spinning with the new information. "That's absolutely horrible."

"It is, dear," she said. "Ivy was such a lovely thing, too. Worked here at camp for a few years before she worked in the field. But really, I shouldn't be telling you any of this."

Mitzi suddenly remembered seeing the name Ivy on the wall of heroes in the main cabin and was filled with a new sadness. She found herself wondering if Alex was involved in this horrible plot, after all. That maybe he was trying to get revenge against camp because of her death.

"Anyway," Ms. Stukes said, snapping Mitzi out of her thoughts, "I can't think of anything you could *give* him, but I bet he would love to come back to a clean health cabin. Just an idea."

"It's a brilliant idea!" Mitzi said enthusiastically. "We are there for jobs, anyway, so we will give the place a good scrub down. Thanks, Ms. Stukes."

"You're welcome, dear," she said as Mitzi raced from the room, dying to give Rose and Finn her new information.

***

"Don't you think it's messed up that Linda didn't tell you about Ivy?" Finn asked as he and Mitzi watched Millie demonstrate the proper way to string a bow.

Mitzi chewed on her cheek, considering his question. "Yes. It's strange that she either didn't think it was important enough to tell us, or didn't think that we should know for some reason."

"Or that she really can't be trusted after all," Finn added.

"Either way," Mitzi said, "it seems as though we finally have a suspect with a possible motive. At least it's *something* to go on."

"True," Finn said. "Better than nothing. Can't wait to hear Rose's take on the whole thing."

They spent the rest of Weapons and Survival class taking turns trying to string a bow, and it proved to be more difficult than Mitzi expected. Finn was able to get it done on his second try, but Mitzi's arms didn't seem strong enough to bend the bow far enough to string it, and it took the rest of the class before she finally got it.

"It's on!" she yelled, almost expecting applause because of how hard it was, but Finn just laughed and shook his head.

"Good," he said. "Now let's go. Rose is waiting at the health cabin by now, I'm sure. That took you an hour."

Mitzi stuck her tongue out playfully. "It did not! You jerk!"

After stopping at the cabinet to put the bow away and scan out of class, Mitzi and Finn sprinted off to the health cabin, where Rose was waiting on the porch.

"About time, you two," she teased, handing her watch to Mitzi. "Let's get to the woods and get this over with."

"Wait until you hear what Mitzi found out," Finn said as he handed Mitzi his watch.

"Spill it, girl," Rose said.

Mitzi looked around and saw a few campers within listening range and, removing her watch, she whispered, "I'll tell you in the woods; too many people out here," as she went inside and tucked the watches under a couch cushion.

They walked the trail to the senior cabin and, after looking carefully around to make sure that no one was watching them, ran around the back of the building to the woods. Mitzi quickly filled Rose in on the lost love of Alex as they pushed their way deeper into the trees.

"Wow!" Rose said. "I don't know what I find more troubling; the fact that Alex could be our bad guy, or that Linda didn't think it was important enough to tell us."

"That's what we thought, too," Finn said.

Mitzi nodded. "So, if Alex is behind the

disappearances, and part of the plot for whatever is going down Friday night, then we really need to figure…"

"Caught ya!" Seph yelled as she and Jeremy stepped out from behind a large tree. "We knew you three were up to something!"

Mitzi was trembling, and annoyed at herself for keeping her guard down. "How much did you hear?"

Jeremy took a step toward them, a look of amusement on his face. "Enough to know that Nurse Alex is some sort of bad guy and Linda didn't tell you about the fact that his girl died."

"Do you think Nurse Alex was one of the men we overheard during midnight mayhem?" Seph asked. "Have those teachers really disappeared?"

"Afraid so," Finn said. "We are trying to find them. Now you know but you can't let this get out.

It would cause a massive panic."

"For sure," Seph said. "How do you know that they didn't just leave?"

"We've checked the marina," Rose said. "There haven't been any boats in or out. No planes either. So unless they can really swim, they're still here."

"Just check the maps," Jeremy suggested, shocking Mitzi that he knew about the maps at all. "If they've removed their watches, they would still leave a heat signature on the map with the thermal filter."

"Don't you think we tried that already?" Rose snapped. "They aren't here. So, we are searching through the woods hoping to…"

"Find their dead bodies?" Seph interrupted, a look of terror on her face.

"Or a cave," Finn said. "Or an underground

hiding spot. Something that would keep them from showing up on the heat scan."

Jeremy scratched his head. "Where have you searched so far? Maybe we can help."

Mitzi was conflicted, happy to have the extra help, but nervous that too many of them would draw unwanted attention. "This is the last bit of forest to search. The only other places left to check are the airstrip fields and the far shoreline."

"What about basements?" Seph said. "Do any of these buildings have basements?"

"As far as I know," Jeremy said as it started to rain, "the only basement is at the radio tower. That's where the island's security center and communication hub is located."

"Jeremy," Seph said, "how about you and I go and check the airstrip while these three keep searching over here?"

"We can't," he said. "We have jobs starting in a few minutes. Besides, we don't have to. I think I might know where they might be hiding."

With that, everyone's attention turned to him. Mitzi was holding her breath and could hardly stand the suspense and blurted, "Well, where do you think they are?"

"A few years back, a bunch of seniors went out to the far shore to party or whatever. They found a bunch of caves and went exploring and the tide rolled in on them, blocking their exit. There was a huge rescue party sent out and, luckily, they were all okay. Since then, the whole area has been off limits to campers. I'd bet anything, they're in one of those sea caves."

"Wouldn't Linda have already sent someone to look there?" Finn said.

"Linda is a ding bat," Seph said. "I don't think

she knows what she's doing half of the time. Probably why SHUT has kept her here for so long."

"Then I guess it's up to us," Mitzi said firmly. "We should go at night. But it may be dangerous. No one has to go if they don't want to."

"Oh, you know I'm in!" Seph blurted.

"Same," chimed in Rose.

Finn and Jeremy nodded.

"It's set then," Mitzi said. "Tonight, we go to the sea caves. Does anyone know when low tide is?"

"I can ask my friend Malakai, down at the marina, and report back at dinner," Finn said. "But what do we do for light? Or weapons?"

"I guess that's where I come in," Jeremy said, shrugging. "I *never* wanted to be the senior captain but I guess it has its benefits." He reached into his pocket and pulled out a fairly large ring of keys, dangling them out, in front of his face.

"They give you the keys?" Mitzi was shocked again.

"Yep," Jeremy said, stuffing the keys back into his pocket. "And one of them is to the weapons and survival cabinet. We can get everything we need in there."

Seph and Jeremy's watches started to buzz.

"Looks like our free time is over and it's time for jobs," Seph whined as she and Jeremy started back. "See you guys at dinner."

"You guys want to just head to the health cabin?" Mitzi asked Finn and Rose. "No point staying out in the rain when there's most likely nothing here anyway."

"Works for me," Rose said as Finn nodded his agreement. "We should make a list of supplies for tonight anyway."

"There may be some stuff in the health cabin

we could bring, too," Mitzi added. "In case anyone needs first aid."

As the three made their way back to the health cabin, Mitzi started to tremble. She couldn't figure out if she was shaking from the wet cold that seemed to have taken permanent residence in her bones, or the fear of what the evening would bring growing like a fire inside of her guts.

Chapter Twenty-Four

At dinner, the five huddled together and very quietly planned their evening mission. Rose gave Jeremy the list of supplies he would gather before the meet up, and Mitzi would bring the first aid supply they had pilfered from the health cabinet. Finn came through with the tide schedule, and low tide was at 2am. After some guesswork, the group decided it would take a good hour to reach the far shore of the island in the dark. The plan was to meet up behind the senior cabin at one, leaving their watches in their cabins, under their pillows.

Lying in bed that night, Mitzi's heart was missing her home. She lay thinking if she could just get word to her father, he would come to their rescue. But she couldn't and the weight of the situation was making her feel sick. It seemed like only moments had passed when she felt Seph's hand gently shaking her shoulder.

It was time. As quietly as she could, Mitzi layered on warm clothes and pulled on her boots, before the two snuck silently out of the cabin. Rose was waiting for them outside, and the three wordlessly took off running across the open field and toward the senior cabin. As they ran, Mitzi looked up at the night sky, happy to find it clear and fairly bright. The moon was almost full.

Finn and Jeremy were waiting for them on the front steps. Jeremy handed each of the girls a flashlight and motioned for them to follow him as he ran to the back of the building.

"No turning back now," Jeremy whispered as he took the first step into the tree line.

They walked without speaking. The only

sounds the snapping of twigs and leaves beneath their feet. After about twenty minutes, Rose broke the silence.

"Are you sure we are going the right way?" she grumbled.

"Yes," Jeremy said. "We are about halfway there, I think. But we shouldn't make any noise. We don't know who is out here."

"Or what," Finn added.

Mitzi hoped that if anything was watching them in the woods, it was a *who* and not a *what*. A chill ran down her spine and she instantly stopped to look around.

"What is it, Mitzi?" Rose whispered.

"I just got the feeling that we are being watched," she said as she shuddered.

"I think we're alone," Seph whispered. "But if someone is watching us, hopefully it's only Linda."

The trees started to space out more and more and, eventually, the group came to the edge of the woods and stood looking out at the rocky shoreline. The moonlight was bright enough to get a basic view of the rocky beach.

Jeremy pointed down to the far end of shoreline where the flat beach transitioned to large rock walls and boulders, barely visible in the darkness. "That's where the caves start, I think."

"We should stick to the tree line to get down there," Mitzi said. "We'd be too exposed on the beach and if anyone came out of one of those caves, they would spot us right away."

"Good thinking, Mitz," Seph said as the made their way down the tree line.

When they had no choice but to head for the rocks, they decided the safest way forward was to split up. That way if one group was caught, the other group could go for help. Mitzi and Jeremy would go first, to scope out the caves, as the other three held back.

The rocks crunched under their feet as they rounded the first boulder, sending chills through Mitzi with each step. If someone was nearby, they would most certainly hear them coming. Mitzi stopped abruptly and grabbed Jeremy's elbow.

"What?" he whispered.

"I think we should have a weapon ready, don't you think?" Mitzi asked. "A few more steps and we will be clearly visible from the caves."

"You're right," he said, digging through his bag and handing her a bright orange gun. "It's a flare gun. The best I could find."

"It should do the trick." Mitzi shrugged, thankful to have some kind of protection. "What about you?"

"I have a large hunting knife and some pepper spray," he said. "I hope we don't need to use any of it."

Mitzi caught a sudden movement near the caves out of the corner of her eye and brought her finger to her lips before pointing it out to Jeremy. Peering carefully around the edge of the boulder, they watched as a man stepped out of the third cave opening. He stood there for several moments, as if he was listening for something. The man turned and started walking down the shore in the opposite direction, and Mitzi and Jeremy stayed completely still for several minutes until he was out of sight completely.

"Was that Alex?" Mitzi asked.

"I think so," Jeremy said, but didn't sound too sure. "I can't say a hundred percent cause it is too dark to make out his face, but I think it *was* him."

"Maybe now is our chance," Mitzi said. "Let's get in there before he comes back."

"Okay," Jeremy agreed. "I just really hope he's working alone and we aren't walking into a certain death."

"Agreed," Mitzi said. "Let's run."

Chapter Twenty-Five

The two sprinted, weapons at the ready, to the mouth of the third cave, and a rush of damp moldy air rushed at them. The entrance was wet—water pooled at their feet—and completely black.

"We will need our flashlights," Mitzi whispered, clicking hers on, careful to shine the beam on the ground.

"Who is there?" a deep voice echoed from inside the cave. "Is someone there? We need help!"

Mitzi and Jeremy looked at each other, frozen with surprise. Jeremy turned his own flashlight on, and stepped into the cold dark opening.

"Please!" another man's panicked voice rang out. "Please help us. Hurry! He may be back soon!"

"We're coming!" Mitzi yelled as they slowly

jogged the unknown and slippery terrain of the sea cave. They soon seemed to be climbing until they came to a chamber. Scanning the room with the flashlights, the breath ran out of Mitzi in horror as her beam settled on a metal cell, set in deep against the darkest corner of the far wall.

As fast as their feet would go, the pair raced to the rusty cell. Mitzi could make out the large form of Instructor Dodge right away and accidentally shone her light directly on his face, causing his eyes to squeeze shut and his face to contort from the sudden bright light.

"Get that light out of my face and get us out of here! You will need to smash the lock!" he yelled, backing away and scrambling over to the motionless lady on the floor that Mitzi assumed was Mrs. Walker. Her heart thumping through her chest, Mitzi moved the flashlight beam around the cell and landed on the large form of Mr. Bell, who was holding his knees and rocking back and forth, mumbling to himself.

"What's wrong with them?" Mitzi asked as Jeremy searched around for something to smash the giant medal padlock.

"He's dehydrated out of his mind," Dodge snapped. "And Mary has been unconscious with fever for over a day. We don't have much time!"

Jeremy returned with a large rock, lifted it high above his head, and struck the lock as hard as he could. The bang reverberated through the cavern, piercing Mitzi's ears, instantly making them ring. After several very loud tries, the lock finally broke free.

Dodge scooped up Mrs. Walker and, carrying her like a baby, stepped out of the cell and turned to Mr. Bell.

"Bell!" he yelled, and Mr. Bell jumped to his trembling feet.

"He'll get us…we can't go…he'll smell us…" Mr. Bell said, visibly shaking with terror stretched across his face.

"Pull yourself together, man!" Dodge hissed. "Come with us now, or stay here to die. The choice is yours. But we gotta leave. Now!"

"This way," Jeremy said, and led Dodge and Mrs. Walker with his flashlight back toward the entrance of the cave, as Mitzi stepped into the cell, taking Mr. Bell by the elbow and slowly leading him out. She would not leave anyone behind.

They made their way slowly. Mitzi could no longer see the beam of Jeremy's flashlight ahead and nervously pushed forward through the darkness. Several very slow minutes later, Mitzi and Mr. Bell stepped out into the fresh island air and Mitzi was instantly calmed in the light of the moon, relieved to see Jeremy running toward them.

"What took you guys so long?" he said, grabbing Mr. Bell's other elbow, pulling them across the rocky beach to the group waiting in the woods.

Dodge, still clutching the unconscious Mrs. Walker, yelled at them as they approached. "Head straight for staff quarters! We've got to get her help and get the camp locked down."

He turned and started off into the woods, but Mitzi yelled, "Wait!"

"What is it?" he yelled back.

"It was Nurse Alex, right?" Mitzi asked. "He's the one that kidnapped you guys, right?"

"Oh man, kid," he said, shaking his head slowly. "You really don't know what we're dealing with here, do you?"

"What do you mean, sir?" Seph asked.

"I don't know what he did, or how he managed to pull it off," Dodge said horridly, "but our precious camp nurse is a damn Vamp."

"Vampire!" Rose and Mitzi shouted at the same time, and the rest were quick to shush them.

"That's right," Dodge said. "We will talk more later. Right now, we need to run. We have to get things ready before that vamp gets back and knows we're out."

The group took off running, led by Jeremy and Dodge, who never stopped to look back. Seph was behind them and every few minutes would stop to let Rose, Mitzi, and Mr. Bell catch up.

"Just leave him," Seph said after waiting for the third time. "He can find his way."

"We can't just leave him," Rose said. "You go on ahead. Mitzi and I will get him there."

Seph shrugged and ran off into the darkness.

But after another very slow twenty minutes, Mitzi was even tempted to leave him. He was still mumbling and his face still glassed over. Thankfully, Dodge came running up with his arms empty and swooped up the plump man, draping him over his back like a rucksack, and took off running. He yelled over his shoulder, "Jeremy and Seph have Mrs. Walker. Now hurry up!"

The cold air burned in Mitzi's chest with each quick breath, her legs burning and feet throbbing, as the senior cabin finally came into view. The group stood at the back of the building, catching their breaths, before they took off around to the front, across the field, and, finally, to the staff house.

Linda was at the door, waving them inside, a frantic look on her face. "Get in! Get in! Oh my God! How did you find them? Get in," she said, slamming the door closed behind the last to enter.

"These kids rescued us," Dodge said, "But how did you know we were coming?"

"I was studying the maps and I saw the kids take off into the forest toward the far shores. I watched them to see what they were doing. Then two of them disappeared from the map, and I waited. After a bit, five thermal signals showed up, so I knew they had found you!" She cleared some papers off her couch and motioned for Jeremy and Seph to put Mrs. Walker down. "You weren't able to save Nurse Alex, too?"

"You mean Vampire Alex," Mitzi said.

"What?" she shrieked. "That's not possible…I mean, are you sure?"

"Oh, we're sure," Dodge said, sitting down in a chair and rubbing his bald head.

The room became so quiet, the only sound was a ticking coming from a clock in the kitchen.

Mitzi looked around at all the faces in the room and couldn't help but wonder how they could possibly fight off an angry vampire.

"We need a plan," Linda said firmly. "And we need it fast."

Chapter Twenty-Six

"So, we are clear on the plan?" Linda asked the worn group as the morning sun came streaming in through her living room window.

"I just hope we are correct in our assumption that Alex is acting alone," Dodge said. "At least until Friday."

"I don't think we have a choice but to assume that," Linda said. "Please stay on full alert during breakfast. Keep your weapons hidden but ready, just in case. I will signal the emergency meeting for all campers in exactly one hour. Dodge will stay here and watch over Mr. Bell and Mary until I return. Stay safe, and I'll see you in an hour. And, kids, make sure you stay together!"

Mitzi nodded and watched as the others did

the same. Stepping out into the cold morning air, Mitzi took a long look around before setting off across the field to the pavilion. It was still very early and only a few campers were already there, quietly enjoying their breakfasts, ignorant to the impending doom surrounding the camp.

"I'm not even hungry," Finn said. "I feel like a zombie."

"I know what you mean," Seph said. "I don't feel like eating either."

Jeremy grabbed a tray. "We need to eat something. We need our strength."

"He's right," Mitzi added. "Who knows when our next real meal is gonna be."

Rose got herself a tray and stood behind Jeremy. "Well, I'm gonna eat 'cuz I'm starving. I've always been a bit of a nervous eater."

After picking up her tray, Mitzi filled it up with

bacon, eggs, and toast. She knew that Jeremy was right. They didn't know what the coming days would bring and this could be their last chance at a hot meal for a while. But she didn't eat much of it. The group sat quietly, as the campers trickled in. Mitzi kept her head on a swivel, as she pushed the eggs around her tray, her insides buzzing on high alert, jumping at every loud noise.

Time was barely moving, and it seemed like they had been sitting there for hours when everyone's watches started buzzing. Mitzi looked at her empty wrist, remembering that hers was still stashed away, but knew the buzzing was the signal for the emergency meeting in the main cabin. She was exhausted, and looking around at her friend's faces, she could clearly see they were tired, too.

"You guys ready for this?" Mitzi asked softly.

"Nope," Rose said.

"Me neither," added Finn.

Seph stood up slowly. "I would rather eat a dog turd," she said.

Jeremy chuckled. "Glad I'm not the only one."

Mitzi blew out a deep breath. "Great!" she said sarcastically. "Let's do this."

***

The main hall was packed and booming with an excited chatter, as Mitzi and her group sat quietly in the front corner of the room. Linda took her place under the giant screen and the voices died away much slower than usual, until, at last, the room was still.

"I'm not going to sugar coat what I am about to tell you all." She stopped and took a slow look around the room. "Camp STASH has been infiltrated by a single Vampire."

Gasps and frantic chatter erupted from the crowd.

"You'll need to be quiet and listen carefully!" she shouted, the room falling silent again. "As you already know, our communications are down so we can't call for help, but we are currently in the process of repairing them. In the meantime, we are on our own and you must follow my instruction implicitly if we are all going to make it through this situation unharmed."

Mitzi took a look around the room, watching the reactions of the other campers, most of which sat unnaturally still and focused on Linda's every word.

"For now, everyone will be on cabin lockdown. Members of Staff as well as Senior Campers will work in shifts standing guard at each cabin, in groups of two. They will be armed and have flares to signal the rest of camp should they run into danger. We will organize food to be brought to your cabins, and will schedule bathroom breaks throughout the day. We will give updates regularly through the radio station. I am asking camper's that have any special weapons training to volunteer for guard as well, but it is not mandatory for you to do so. Extra guards will be located at staff quarters and in the radio tower.

"Looking out at your faces, I see that several of you are frightened. Please be assured, as long as you follow the rules, you will be safe and help will be on the way soon enough. When this meeting is over, unless you are volunteering for guard duty, you need to return to your cabins, as a group, and stay there until further instruction. Meeting adjourned."

Like a stampede of elephants, campers rushed out of the room, leaving only a dozen or so students hanging behind. Mitzi's heart skipped a beat at the sight of Trent still sitting at his spot on the floor and wondered why he would be volunteering. She also noticed a terrified looking Millie, now pacing the floor and mumbling to herself. There were a few others, who Mitzi didn't know, and the five of them.

"Seph and Millie," Linda said, pointing to each of them. "You are both skilled archers if I remember correctly."

"Yes ma'am," Seph said as Millie nodded.

"You take first shift in the radio tower. Gather supplies quickly and stay together. Remember, you'll need garnet tipped arrows."

"I hope we don't actually need them," Millie said, her voice trembling.

"It's just a precaution," Linda said. "Now go!"

Linda sent a few other campers to guard the marina, and another pair to the staff building, before turning to face Trent. Mitzi held her breath, dying to hear what he was volunteering for exactly.

"And what is your skill set, young man?"

Linda asked him. "What help can you offer?"

"I'm not sure, really," he said quietly, "but I am pretty good with technology. My dad has taught me a lot, so I thought maybe I could take a look at the communications mess and see if I can help get them back up and running."

"Oh!" Linda said as realization swept over her face, "Your father created AIDA, right?"

Trent nodded.

"Good," Linda said, pointing to Rose. "You go together and tell them I sent you. It's in the basement of the radio tower. Go."

Rose and Trent stood up and walked out, Rose turning to make eye contact with Mitzi, who gave her a quick thumbs up before shifting her attention back to Linda.

"Jeremy," she said. "I need you on first watch at senior cabin; there will be a member of staff meeting you there. Please run. You will be alone until you get there."

"Finn and Mitzi," she said, taking in a big breath and very slowly exhaling. "I want you two to stay with me. We have some gear to distribute."

With the news, Mitzi was suddenly aware of the fatigue setting into her bones but tried to shake it off. There would be time to rest soon enough.

"Let's go," Linda said, and sped out of the room, a sleepy but determined Finn and Mitzi, following behind her.

Chapter Twenty-Seven

Mitzi and Finn spent the next few hours driving around the camp delivering supplies to each lookout station. The supplies themselves were pretty basic. A walkie-talkie, can of pepper spray, hunting knife, and a bow with four arrows was handed to each pair of guards.

"It sure would be nice if the camp had some guns," Finn complained as the golf cart sped toward the staff house after their final delivery.

"We have never needed any," Linda said defensively. "This is a training camp with the highest security protocols in the world. Nothing like this has ever happened before. We will make do with the weapons that we have."

"If Alex is a vampire," Mitzi asked, "how did

he get into camp in the first place?"

"That was troubling me, too, Mitzi," Linda said. "I spent an hour scouring my reference books and the only thing that makes sense is that he was bitten within about twenty-four hours of arriving. That's the only way he could have made it through security on arrival. Apparently, it takes a full day for the transition to be detectable, once bitten. He had a slight fever when he arrived, but he said he was just getting over a bug and we thought nothing of it."

"What if he isn't the only one who got through security? What if we have more Vamps among us that got in the same way?" asked Finn as the cart came to a stop in front of the staff house.

"I was worried about the same thing," said Linda, "so I checked and then re-checked that every staff member and camper has a glowing heat signature on the map. Every single member of my staff, and every single camper, has been checked and verified, twice."

Mitzi stood and stretched, her muscles aching from the damp. "Could there be more Vampires here, though?" she asked. "Could he have somehow let some in? They wouldn't show up on the map, right?"

"You do ask very good questions," Linda said as she walked to the door, motioning for them to follow. "If he did, I don't know how he could have done it. Our shorelines have a laser grid alarm barrier, which is still perfectly operational. I really believe that Alex is working alone, but I am concerned about Friday."

The three entered Linda's apartment and found Dodge sitting alone in the living room.

"I put Mary in your bed," he said to Linda. "Her fever is finally coming down and I think she will be okay."

Linda nodded. "And Mr. Bell?"

"I fed him and brought him upstairs to his apartment," he said. "He fell asleep as soon as his head hit his pillow."

"Thank you, Dodge," she said. "Why don't you go get a couple hours of sleep? I'll need you fresh for the evening."

"Okay, Linda," he said as he stood and walked to the door. He paused with his hand on the doorknob and turned his head just enough to look at Mitzi and Finn. "By the way, kids," he said softly, "I never said thank you for saving our lives."

Mitzi could feel her face burn and she shifted her weight. "You don't have to thank us."

"Yes, I do," he said firmly. "Thank you."

***

After Dodge left, Linda sent Mitzi and Finn

back to their cabins to get some rest. She told them she would send for them if they were needed. They walked to the cabins quietly, too tired to speak. Mitzi needed sleep, and disappointment rushed through her when she stepped inside cabin four. It sounded like a circus. She didn't think that she would be able to sleep in all the noise but decided to try anyway, hoping that no one would notice her come in, too tired for any questions.

She felt guilty going to bed, seeing Seph and Millie's beds empty, knowing they were still working, but knew she would be more useful overall if she got some sleep. Quietly climbing up, she snuggled under her blankets, fully clothed, and, lying on her side, put her pillow over her head to shield the light and noise.

She worried that it was still too loud, and that she would never fall asleep. But then the sounds became a backdrop, tunneling further and further away, until, at last, they faded into silence.

Chapter Twenty-Eight

Mitzi was startled awake by someone pulling the pillow slowly off her face and sat up in a flash, heart pounding and looking around frantically. "What's happening?" she asked.

"I'm sorry that I scared you," Seph said, standing next to her. "You slept through lunch and they are bringing dinner in. I thought you should probably eat something."

"I slept through lunch!" Mitzi exclaimed, feeling a rush of embarrassment.

"Don't feel bad," Seph shrugged. "Millie and I got in shortly after you, and we both just woke up, too. You just missed Millie. She went back to the tower to stand watch. She is hardcore!"

Mitzi felt a twang of guilt, knowing that Millie

was already back out on watch, but also a little better, knowing she wasn't the only one to have slept. "Is there any news?"

"Actually, yes," Seph said. "When I finished my watch shift, Linda told me that tonight a few of the adults are going to go and try to capture Alex. We are going on the offensive."

"Oh man," Mitzi groaned. "Who is going? Did she say?"

"Dodge, Mr. Ross, and two of the security dudes," she said.

"Do you think they will be able to catch him?" Mitzi asked, suddenly wishing she could talk to Finn and Rose about the whole thing.

"It's hard to say," she said, sitting down on the edge of her bed. "Vamps are so fast. They would really need to catch him by surprise."

Mitzi plopped back on her pillow and let out a

big sigh. "We need to get a call out for help," she said. "Have they gotten anywhere with fixing the coms yet?"

"No," Seph said softly. "And the weather is still too rough to send out a boat. The good news is that Linda thinks they found the problem and they may be able to have the coms back up and running by the morning."

"That's great news!" Mitzi said, propping herself up onto her elbows. "I just hope that whoever answers our call for help, can get here on time."

"Line up and get your dinner!" a male voice shouted from behind, spinning Mitzi around in her bed. She hadn't even heard the door open. Two senior campers, each holding a large box filled with brown bags, stood by the door as the campers lined up.

Seph got up and, forgoing the line, walked

straight over and, nodding at one of the boys, snatched two bags and threw one to Mitzi.

"What do you think?" she said. "Steak and Lobster tail?"

Mitzi jiggled her bag, playing along. "Feels more like pizza and wings to me."

Mitzi watched as Seph rolled open her bag and looked inside. "Dang. Looks like PB and J. I honestly don't know how they expect us to survive."

Mitzi smiled, happy for the food, but then a realization made her smile fall.

"What's the matter?" Seph asked.

"We are no closer to knowing what is going to happen tomorrow and I'm scared," she admitted. "How are we supposed to protect ourselves when we don't really know what we are up against?"

Seph sat nibbling on her sandwich as Mitzi waited for her to answer. She took a long slurp from her juice box and then looked up at Mitzi.

"Maybe we aren't in any *grave* danger," Seph said as Mitzi flashed her a look of confusion. "If Alex wanted to kill anyone, he would have killed the teachers, but instead he just locked them up, right?"

"That is true," Mitzi said. "But what if he was saving them for someone else to kill?"

"I didn't think of that," Seph admitted. "Now you got me all worried again."

"Sorry," Mitzi said. "I just feel so hopeless just sitting here. I want to be out helping. I'll go crazy siting here all night!"

"Linda said she would call us in the morning and we just have to sit tight for now," Seph said as she crumbled her empty brown bag. "I don't know about you, but I have a feeling this is gonna be a long night."

***

And it was a long night. Thankfully, after dinner, some seniors dropped by with a big box full of cards, board games, books, and drawing supplies. Mitzi and Seph spent several hours on her top bunk playing go fish and war, and Seph even taught her a game called six card. At eight o'clock, they started giving groups of six campers at a time bathroom breaks, and an announcement came afterward, telling them a bucket would be dropped off in case anyone needed to use the bathroom in the night.

Millie returned to the cabin, right before lights out, holding a bucket and roll of toilet paper and set them in the corner of the room. She looked drained and pale but Mitzi was hopeful she would be able to give them an update.

It wasn't the update that Mitzi was hoping for.

"They couldn't find him," Millie said, dropping onto her bed like a sack of potatoes. "They looked everywhere. There's another group going out in the morning but, for now, we're just gonna hold tight for the night."

"Hold tight?" Seph whined. "I'm not gonna sleep a wink tonight."

"I don't think I will either," Mitzi agreed.

Millie kicked off her shoes and crawled under her covers. "I won't have that problem. Every cabin has two armed guards, all night. Get some sleep, girls."

As the cabin lights turned off automatically, Mitzi could see the beams of a dozen or so flashlights popping on throughout the room. Seph was back in her own bunk, shining hers above her head, eyes wide awake.

Mitzi lay there, trying not to worry about the vampire, hiding out in the darkness, or what evil may have been coming their way. She closed her eyes, listening to the whispers and occasional giggles of other campers, wishing she could be more like them. It was like they weren't even scared. It was like a game to them. They didn't seem to understand the gravity of the situation, and maybe that was a good thing. It must have been nice to not worry. But then again, most of these kids hadn't seen the things Mitzi had seen. Images of mimic blobs, Vampires, and werewolves flashed through Mitzi's mind, playing like a short film set on repeat. But despite the troubles of her mind, she managed to drift off.

Chapter Twenty-Nine

Mitzi's eyes popped open. Her heart was pounding. Something was watching her. She tried to sit up but couldn't. She tried to speak but no sound would come out. She darted her eyes around the room, terrified. She wasn't sure if she was dreaming or awake. She could hear several cries break out around the room and wanted to cry out, too. She needed help. Something invisible was holding her down. She tried to scream again, but ... nothing.

"Mitzi!" Seph yelled out, and flashed her beam of light on top of her, releasing what it was that had a hold on her. Mitzi sat up, covered in a cold sweat, and noticed a dark form in the far corner. "There!" she yelled, pointing at the shadow.

Seph swept her beam in the direction Mitzi

pointed and they caught the smallest glimpse of a man's dark shape running from the light, just a shadow, darker than anything around it.

"There!" another camper yelled, pointing, and Seph and several others shined their lights and saw two dark man-shaped forms, this time barely escaping the light, and as the girls tried to get the beams on them, they would just miss.

A deep and sinister laugh filled the cabin, seeming to come from every corner of the room. Several campers were crying, clinging to each other in the dark, unsure of what to do.

"Everyone get in the center of the room and shine your flashlights out!" Mitzi yelled as dozens of terrified campers did as she said. Seph bravely ran to the door and opened it, yelling, "Get these lights on now! There are Shadow Men in here!"

The girls stayed huddled in the center of the

room as the dark laughter continued, growing louder and louder. Beams of light shooting out from the girls like a crazy disco ball could not seem to land on one of the figures. The laughter was growing so loud it was starting to hurt Mitzi's ears.

Snap. The lights came on and the laughter stopped instantly. Mitzi looked around at the terrified and tear-covered faces of the other campers. No one moved. Many of them shaking, afraid.

"Don't worry, girls," Seph said. "They can't come back with the lights on. I'll make sure these lights stay on, I promise. Come on, Mitzi."

Mitzi and Seph got outside just as Linda and Dodge were zooming up in the golf cart to meet with the two seniors that were standing guard.

Linda glanced up at Mitzi. "You girls should be inside. What are you doing out here?"

Ignoring her completely, Seph asked, "Is it just

our cabin? Or are they everywhere?"

"They have attacked all four cabins," she said. "How many do you think you had in there, Seph?"

"Three for sure," she said. "Probably more. But, you can't turn those lights off again. I promised the girls."

"I wouldn't dream of it, Seph."

"How did they get here?" Mitzi asked.

"I don't know how they got here. They must have been called here. The bigger questions are, what do they want and how do we get rid of them?"

"They want what all Shadow Men want. Our souls," Seph said. "Taking bits of human souls is how they get stronger."

"I know that," Linda said with growing frustration. "I mean, what do they want at camp, all of a sudden? Why are they here?"

"I have a theory," Mitzi said softly. "Maybe

they want the Covenant Cube. Their blood vial is the only one still in SHUT's possession."

"It isn't *here,* though!" Dodge said. "Why would they come here?"

"Maybe to hold us as prisoners? Until it's given to them?" Seph said.

Linda sighed. "I guess that's one possibility."

"I hate to say it, but," Mitzi said, "if Alex is a vamp and he's working with the Shadow Men, who's to say he isn't working with the werewolves as well? Maybe that's what will show up tomorrow somehow. They only need that last vial to release the dark trinity. Maybe they plan on trading us, for the vial."

"Mitzi, I really hope you are wrong about this but I'm afraid you may be right. You know why?" Linda said as she rubbed small circles on the sides of her forehead. "Because tomorrow night is a full moon. I don't think that's a coincidence."

"What are we gonna do, Linda?" Dodge asked. "We aren't equipped to fight off Vampires, werewolves, and Shadow Men? This is crazy!"

"We have *got* to call for help," Linda said firmly. "We will go check on coms; they might be fixed very soon. Then I will call an emergency gathering in the fields at sunrise. We just need to keep everyone calm for now until we can come up with some kind of plan."

"What do you want us to tell the girls?" Seph said, pointing to the cabin behind her. "They are totally freaking out. We gotta tell 'em something."

"Just tell them that the lights will remain on and that everyone is safe for now." Linda put her hand on Seph's shoulder. "I need you to reassure them that we will keep them safe, because, Seph, we *will* keep you all safe."

"We need to move," Dodge grumbled. "We

have to check on the other cabins and get over to check coms. It will be sun up before we know it and we need a plan."

"Right," Linda said, nodding slightly while making quick eye contact with Mitzi and then Seph. "Let's go."

Chapter Thirty

The entire camp was huddled together in the center of the field, the air was dense with fog, and the morning sun provided very little warmth as they sat awaiting further instruction. The adults and several of the seniors, including Jeremy, stood armed, facing outward, forming a perimeter around the swarm of quiet campers. Mitzi glanced over at Rose and Finn, giving them a nervous smile. Seph and Millie were sitting close behind them, looking just as nervous and tired as everyone else.

The hum of the golf cart could be heard making its way to the crowd, and Mitzi watched as it broke through the fog and came to a stop in front of them. Doge and Linda got out and Linda cleared her throat as she scanned the audience before her.

"Campers," she said boldly, "as you all know by now, we are faced with an unprecedented situation. Camp STASH is under attack." Her voice reverberated in the field and Mitzi could feel her words echo through her body.

"Today," Linda said, "you are no longer just campers. Today, you must take on the role of Hunters and prove to yourselves that you can handle the dangers of the world around you."

Several cries and nervous chatter broke out around the crowd.

"You *must* dig deep, putting away your fears, and focus on the courage within you. I know that many of you are new. Many of you have only learned of SHUT a few short weeks ago and this is both overwhelming and terrifying, but be rest assured, you were born for this and good will prevail.

"With this horrific situation, comes a ray of

light. Our security team, with the help of a very tech savvy camper, are fairly certain they will have communications up and running within the next several hours. We will call for outside help the moment we are able to. Please remember, the Shadow Men that invaded our cabins last night are powerless in the light. We will spend our day preparing for whatever nightfall may bring.

"We do have a supply plane landing at three this afternoon. That plane is either our ticket to salvation, or part of the plot to destroy us. We just have no way of knowing which, until it arrives. We will be prepared for either possibility.

"First time campers, you will be stationed in the main cabin today. You will be tasked with preparing the building for tonight. Mr. Ross and three seniors will be your team leaders. You will secure the building and make it battle ready.

"Now, go," she said, pointing toward the main cabin. "Food will be delivered to you all later. If you are needed, you will be sent for." She slightly nodded and made eye contact with Mitzi as she stood with the other first year campers, leaving Seph sitting alone.

"You guys be safe," Seph whispered. "I'm sure I'll see you soon."

"I wish you were coming with us," Finn said, cheeks blazing.

Seph smiled at him, making his cheeks even more red. "Me, too, Finn."

Rose looked at Mitzi and gave her a look that asked, 'what's that all about?' but Mitzi was equally confused and just shrugged.

"You stay safe, too. Don't be a hero," Mitzi said as they walked off with their group.

"Like you could talk!" Seph shouted after her.

As they walked through the fog, Mitzi hung back a bit, trying to hear what Linda was saying to the rest of the group. But between the chatter of kids and the thickness of the fog, she couldn't make out anything at all. She would just have to wait and she really hated waiting.

Chapter Thirty-One

The moment they arrived in the main cabin, they found a huge pile of supplies waiting for them in the center of the room. Mr. Ross broke the campers into groups of eight or ten, and assigned each group a specific duty. The first group had to hang the dozen powerful UV lights, both inside and outside of the building, connected to the generator, in case the power was cut. When turned on, they would be bright enough to burn any vampire, and would definitely keep the Shadow Men at a safe distance.

Group two had the task of filling the camp's entire arsenal of water guns and water balloons with a mixture of holy water and sterling silver dust, a painful concoction for any werewolf or demon.

The third group was tasked with setting up a laser perimeter around the building that would set off an alarm inside if crossed.

The fourth were charged with lining the window sills and doorways with salt as well as setting a second perimeter around the building with a thick line of salt. Salt was no good at keeping the Vamps and werewolves out, but may keep the Shadow Men at bay.

Mitzi's group, the last group, was tasked with collecting thick sticks and small branches from around the cabin and carving them into as many stakes as possible. After collecting them, the eight campers sat in a circle, carving the tips into a sharp point.

"That makes nine," Finn said, looking pleased with himself as he set another completed stake into his pile.

Rose rolled her eyes. "For crying out loud, Finn. It's not a competition."

"Besides," a boy said from across the circle, "you wouldn't win anyway. I just finished my eleventh one."

"Can we just focus on what we're doing and have some quiet?" Mimi said as she struggled to carve her third stick. "This whole thing is making me a nervous wreck!"

"Let's just hope we don't have to actually use these," Anya chimed in. "Can you imagine trying to stab a vamp in the chest with one of these?"

Mitzi shuddered. Not only did she think she *couldn't* do it, but the thought of being close enough to an attacking vampire to need to absolutely terrified her.

The boy across the circle set another finished stake in his pile. "I just don't get it," he said. "Why are half of us preparing for Vamps and the other half preparing for werewolves? I thought the only threat was one vampire and the Shadow Men. I'm so confused."

"Me too," said the unknown girl, sitting to his left.

Mitzi looked from Finn to Rose and hoped they would answer, but when neither of them did, she said, "It's because they don't know what's coming. All they know is that something is happening tonight, and that whatever it is, seems to be a coordinated effort of at least one vampire and several Shadow Men."

"And tonight is a full moon," Finn added. "So, if the theories are correct, and something is going down at camp tonight, there's a good chance it has to do with werewolves."

The boy shook his head. "I really hope the

theories are wrong then."

"We all do," Mitzi said.

They group carved in silence after that. Mr. Ross came by and said they had enough and told them to stack them up inside and wait for lunch to arrive. The rest of the campers were starting to arrive at the main cabin to hunker down until further instruction. The cabin was packed. Almost every inch of floor, taken by an exhausted looking Camper. Mitzi scanned the room, but didn't see Seph anywhere, and wondered if she was assigned another task.

Mitzi's hands and back were sore from carving and sitting on the damp ground for so long. After stacking up the stakes inside, she found an unoccupied corner to sit and relax against the wall with Finn and Rose. It was a welcome break. It was just a few minutes later when lunch arrived. Ham and cheese sandwiches and a bag of chips never tasted so good. The red sports drink was a nice treat, too.

"That really hit the spot," Finn said, crumbling up his empty food bag.

"Yeah, it was good, but now what?" Rose asked. "Are we supposed to just sit here and wait?"

"Oh God, I hope not," Mitzi said.

But that was exactly what they had to do. Wait. And wait. And wait. The first hour, the room was abuzz with energetic chattering. The second hour brought a shift in the mood, as the campers were getting restless, and grouchy, complaining. By the end of the third hour, most of the crowd had fallen asleep, curled up blanket less on the floor or huddled against a friend. The room was eerily quiet. So quiet that Mitzi could hear the buzz of an airplane overhead. She looked up at the ceiling, straining to hear it.

"It's time, then huh?" Finn glanced up at the ceiling. "I hope that captain Frank is alright. He seemed like such a nice guy."

"I just hope that no one gets hurt," Mitzi said, and ran her fingers through her hair. "And I really I wish I knew what was happening. This not knowing is driving me crazy!"

"Don't worry, Mitz," Finn said. "We will know soon enough."

Chapter Thirty-Two

Mitzi looked up and was surprised to see Mr. Ross walking across the room toward her, stepping carefully between the campers on the floor. Something was up. She could tell by the strained expression on his face, and he seemed to be avoiding eye contact with her.

"Mitzi," he said softly. "You have been called to the staff house. Take these two with you." He nodded at Finn and Rose before quickly turning to walk away.

A shiver ran through Mitzi as the three stood. "You guys ready for this? Cuz I'm not," she admitted.

"Girl, I'm never ready for this stuff, you know that," Rose said, stretching her arms above her head.

"I'm as ready as I'm gonna be," Finn added.

"Just wish Mr. Ross gave us a little more info is all."

The three made their way out, single file, stepping over and around the campers that, to Mitzi, reminded her of sitting ducks. It had started to rain again, but at least it wasn't a heavy rain so they didn't get completely soaked on their short run over to the staff house.

Linda was waiting at the door when they arrived, and brushed them quickly inside, closing the door behind them. Inside Linda's apartment, Mitzi was surprised to see Captain Frank, sitting between Dodge and another unfamiliar man on the couch. Linda motioned for the kids to sit in the chairs set opposite the couch and then took a seat in the big chair at the other end.

"Kids, you all know Captain Frank," Linda said, "and this here is Joe. He's one of our camp security guards."

Mitzi nodded at the men, confused with why she was asked to come. She noticed that Linda's hands were trembling and Dodge seemed off, his shoulders slumped, his eyes sad and staring at the floor. Captain Frank's eyes were wide and darting around the room like he was expecting something to jump out and yell "boo" at any moment. Joe was expressionless.

"First of all, I need to know if you know anything about the whereabouts of three missing campers," Linda asked, staring Mitzi straight in the eyes.

"What?" Mitzi was shocked. "Who is missing?"

"Seph, who I know is a friend of yours," she said as Finn let out an involuntary gasp, sitting up straighter in his chair. "And two boys, Jeremy Wright and Malakai Alexander. I need to know if you know anything about this at all."

"I don't!" Mitzi said. "Do you think they've been taken?"

"I don't think so, no," she said. "There is a boat missing from the marina. We think they took it. Malakai is one of only three students with access to the dock locking systems."

"That makes sense," Rose said. "I bet they went for help. Seph told me that she thought someone should take a boat for help and couldn't understand what you were all waiting for."

"Stupid fools!" Linda shouted. "They will get themselves killed out there and there is nothing we can do to help them right now."

Mitzi could feel her heart pounding in her ears. She blinked her eyes several times to fight back the tears that were starting to pool. What had Seph, Jeremy, and Malakai gotten themselves into? *What if they can't make it?*

"As horrible as that all is," Linda said, "the rest of what I have to tell you is even worse."

The room was so quiet all that Mitzi could hear was a steady *tick tick tick* from the clock in the kitchen and a light *tap tap tap* of the rain drumming on the roof.

"Dodge and Joe watched from the tree line as the supply plane landed. Now, normally, during a supply run, two people meet the plane to verify the packing list and sign off on the shipment, then it's off-loaded onto a utility cart and driven back to camp.

"We, of course, didn't know what was on the plane, but we also didn't know if whatever was on the plane was in contact with Alex and would be ready to attack. After careful consideration, we decided to act like nothing was out of the ordinary and to proceed as we usually do…but heavily armed, of course, and with a tree line full of fighters at the ready, should anything go wrong."

"Dodge, you can take it from here?" Linda asked as Dodge leaned back and let out a giant sigh.

"So, we approach and Captain Frank is his usual chipper self. He says hello and he is opening up the cargo door. That's when I grabbed him and took him to the front of the plane and told him he might have something other than our order on board."

"I can still hardly believe it," Captain Frank mumbled.

"He was shocked, of course, and I asked him to call for help, which he promptly did. While he was back inside the cockpit, making the radio call, I leaned my head inside and said, 'We know you're in there and we have you surrounded. Why don't you just give yourselves up now'."

Dodge put his face in his hands.

"Then what happened?" Finn blurted.

"One of them answered," Joe said. "Weirdest crap I have ever heard."

Mitzi looked at Rose and Finn, who looked just as perplexed as she felt.

Dodge sat up to explain. "It answered in a song. Something I think I will remember forever,

'The darkness is already here, there's nothing you can do,

We will eat your happiness and your family, too,

You can't run and you can't hide, we're everywhere you go.

When the lights go out tonight…' Ummm, I can't say the last line out loud," he said, shaking his head.

"That's when the blood will flow," Joe said.

"Then it laughed. But several other laughs joined in and the door slammed shut on its own. I nearly had a heart attack."

"Then what did you do?" Rose asked.

"We grabbed Captain Frank and ran for it," Dodge said. "But all of a sudden, there was a swooshing noise and smack dab, right in our path, Alex stood. Fangs out with bloodshot eyes. We froze in a faceoff. Him against the three of us. I tried reaching into my pocket but in a flash, he grabbed my neck and he hissed out a few words and zoom, he was gone."

"I know I'm going to regret asking this, but what did he say?" Mitzi asked.

Dodge rubbed his face hard and looked at Linda. He clearly didn't want to be the one to say the words out loud.

Linda sighed. "He said 'deliver Mitzi Clark or

everyone dies'."

The air was sucked out of the room, and Mitzi's face went cold. Linda looked at Mitzi's pale face and said, "Don't worry, dear. We won't…"

But Mitzi couldn't hear her words as the room went black and spiraled and spun into complete darkness as she fell out of her chair and onto the floor.

Chapter Thirty-Three

"Mitzi! Mitzi!"

Mitzi cracked her eyes open to find herself lying on the floor with Rose leaning over her. Her head was throbbing and she was confused, and as she sat up, a wave of realization hit her.

"Oh my God, girl, are you alright?" Rose said, pulling her up slowly onto her chair. "You passed out!"

"I don't know what happened," Mitzi said. "I never passed out before. Why do they want me? What do they want with me?"

Linda showed up next to Mitzi and handed her a glass of water. "Best we figure is they want to use you as a bargaining tool to get the last vial of the Covenant Cube."

"But why all of the theatrics?" Mitzi said as the tears were building in her eyes. "Why didn't they just take me at home? Kidnap me? Why here at camp? Why didn't Alex just take me?"

"I think it's a show of force," Dodge answered as tears rolled down Mitzi's face. "They want to show SHUT how powerful they are."

"So what do we do?" Rose said. "We aren't just gonna hand Mitzi over to them."

"Of course we aren't," Linda said. "We just need to stall them. Captain Frank was able to get a call for help out. Member of SHUT should be here within a few hours. We will just need to stall until then."

"That's right," Captain Frank said. "What if we get Mitzi on the plane and I fly her out of here? They would leave, right?"

"I don't think they will let that plane out of

their sights, and I think that would be too risky anyway," Dodge said.

"Plus, we still have no idea exactly who and what we're up against," Joe said. "It could be three or four werewolves, or it could be ten. We have no idea."

"I am confused about one thing," Finn said, and everyone turned to look at him. "How did you not know you had people on board, Captain Frank? I mean, when did they get on? It's not a very big plane. Aren't there weight restrictions and stuff?"

Everyone turned to Captain Frank, awaiting his explanation.

"I...I.." he stuttered nervously, darting his eyes from person to person. "I was running late to the airport! The plane was already loaded. It's *always* already loaded! I didn't look at the manifest. I've done the trip so many times I was just in a hurry and skipped over it. I should have looked! I'm sorry. Really, I am!" His face contorted with guilt and he covered his face with his hands.

Mitzi watched his shoulders tremble with grief and believed that he was telling the truth, but Finn was not so easily convinced.

"Wasn't the plane flying differently, though?" he said. "That's a lot more weight than you're used to. Especially having flown the trip, as you said, so many times?"

His hands dropped and revealed his tear-streaked face. He looked directly at Finn and spoke softly. "Honestly, son, nothing seemed different at all. It was just like any other flight here. Honest."

Finn bit his fingernail, quietly considering the pilot's explanation, before slowly nodding his approval of the pilot's story. "So, how do we stall these monsters before the help arrives?" he asked.

"Everyone needs to get into the main hall," Linda said, jumping to her feet. "That's our best chance. We will keep the plane surrounded with as many armed volunteers and staff as possible. I'll get over to the tower and see if we have patched communications yet. Find out exactly when help will arrive."

"And then?" Dodge asked.

"Then, we wait," said Linda. "Or we fight. But I hope it won't come to that."

"Sitting ducks," Mitzi said.

"What was that, Mitzi?" Linda asked.

"Aren't we just sitting ducks all piled into one building? Shouldn't we spread out or something?" Mitzi asked, and Rose added "That's a good point."

"Normally, I would agree with you, Mitzi," Linda said. "But we have over a hundred kids here that have never even seen a monster yet, much less had to fight one. I really think our best chance at keeping everyone safe is by staying together and protecting each other the best we can."

Mitzi nodded. "Then what are we waiting for? Let's move."

Chapter Thirty-Four

Night was closing in. The main cabin was quiet and packed with wide-eyed children sitting back-to-back, and shoulder-to-shoulder, jumping at the slightest sound. Mr. Ross who was pacing the front wall, stopping to peer out of the front windows every few moments, looked as though he was running on empty. Mitzi sat still, squeezing Rose's hand and pressed against Finn's side, unable to shift her focus from listening to any signs of trouble.

The door flew open and Linda, soaked from the rain, stepped in and addressed the room. "They're coming."

Cries broke out around the room as everyone scrambled to their feet, several kids hugging each other in fear, many arming themselves with stakes, rushing to the windows to try to get a glance of the enemy at their doorstep.

Mitzi, Finn, and Rose ran over to Linda.

"How many are there?" Mitzi asked. "Did you get hold of our rescue team to find out when they will arrive?"

"Coms are still down. They're doing everything they can. It looks like we are up against four werewolves and at least one Vamp. The heat maps don't show the Vamps so there could be more. But they are definitely coming our way. So, be ready."

"I want to fight, too," Mitzi said, surprised by the words coming out of her own mouth. "I don't want to just wait in here while everyone is fighting for our lives out there."

"It's just too dangerous, Mitzi," she said as she put a hand on her shoulder. "I need you three in here. Protect these kids should the worst happen and they manage to get through."

Mitzi nodded. She wanted to argue. She felt responsible for this mess somehow and thought she should be out there, trying to stop it. But she also knew there wasn't much she could do anyway. The only monster that she ever had to fight was a slow-moving mimic. Vampires and werewolves were a whole different story.

"Then we will stand guard on the porch," she demanded, not sure if Linda would agree.

"I guess that will do," Linda agreed. "But not one step off the porch! Understood?"

"Understood," Mitzi said as Finn and Rose nodded their agreement. They followed Linda out and watched as she ran toward the staff and students standing guard, taking her place beside them.

"Look," Rose said, and pointed out across the field. In the distance, Mitzi could just make out the dark forms of several human-like figures, fanned out and closing in on them.

"There's eight of them!" Finn said. "Four and four, I would guess."

Mitzi picked up a wooden stake and slapped it in her hand, glaring out at the fields. "Grab a weapon, you two. It's about to get real."

***

As the line of attackers got closer, Mitzi watched as the several brave defenders shifted their stances, bringing various weapons over their heads, ready to attack. Linda, Dodge, and Captain Frank stood near the center of the group and Dodge was swinging a chain attached to a pointed metal spikey ball at the end of it, circling it over his head as he yelled out to the monsters, "Leave here now! Or there will be hell to pay!"

But a gravely and sinister voice returned his

call with, "We only want the girl. Give her to us and we will be on our way."

Linda took a step toward the monsters, who were now close enough to them for Mitzi to see more clearly. It was easy to tell the werewolves apart from the Vampires. The werewolves were filthy, dressed in layers of torn clothes, with broken and missing teeth and long, stringy, and wild hair. The Vampires, on the other hand, were clean-cut, well-dressed, and, other than seeming a bit twitchy and nervous, they looked like regular people. At least they did when they weren't baring their fangs. Seeing Alex there as one of them made Mitzi sick to her stomach. Why would he have done this?

"What do you want with the girl?" Linda demanded bravely. "If we hand her over to you, how do we know you will keep your word and no one will get hurt?"

Mitzi watched as the tall werewolf stepped closer to Linda and growled at her. "You don't. But you should know that if we wanted you dead, you would all be dead already."

With that, the four Vampires, Alex included, bared their fangs and hissed at Linda, and the other three werewolves laughed evil laughter.

"The full moon is on the rise," the tall werewolf snapped, pointing a bony finger toward the sky. "You know there is no way to stop us once we transition. If you don't want a bloodbath on your hands, just give us the girl now, before it's too late."

"But what do you want with her?" Linda asked.

"She is the key to getting what we need," he answered.

"So you plan to trade her for the Shadow Man's blood vial then. Just as we thought," Dodge said, still swinging his weapon. "SHUT will never let you have it."

"Oh, yes they will," he snarled.

Captain Frank, gripping a stake in his hands, stepped closer to Linda. "What makes you think they would trade the vial for the girl?"

The monster looked Captain Frank over slowly, from head to foot. "You'd be surprised what a father will do for his daughter," the werewolf laughed, "or so I've been told."

"Ben Clark will never give you the vial," Linda said. "Give up on this nonsense now."

"Enough of this chatter!" Alex yelled, and everyone turned to look at him. "You have one hour to give up the girl. Or we will come and take her."

Alex turned and left in a flash of dust, and the three others zoomed away right after him.

"You heard the Vamp, the fast devils, they

are," the tall werewolf said. "You have one hour."

The four werewolves moved away slowly, walking backward through the field, smiling and sneering, until when they were almost out of sight, they turned and ran into the woods as the darkness of night descended onto the camp.

Linda turned to Captain Frank. "Do you think the help will arrive within the hour?"

"They should be here very soon," he said. "I made that call a while ago."

Linda said something back to Captain Frank, but Mitzi couldn't quite make it out from her spot on the porch. She watched as Dodge and Frank came toward her as Linda took off with another camper toward the tower.

"Linda is checking coms again," Dodge said. "Hopefully, she will have some good news for us."

Frank shifted and grabbed his stomach. "I

need to go to the bathroom. When I get upset, there's just no stopping my guts."

"Ewe," Rose said.

"Well, you can't go alone," Dodge said. "Too dangerous."

"I can take the kid," he said, nodding at Finn.

"I have a name, you know." Finn rolled his eyes and looked over at Mitzi, who smiled at him. "It's Finn."

"Sorry, Finn," he said. "Don't mind me. I'm not myself."

Finn shrugged. "None of us are. Let's go." Finn grabbed a stake and small silver-powder and water filled water gun, and shuffled down the steps, followed by a pale a sweaty Frank.

"With that look on poor Captain Frank's face," Rose said, "they may be a while. Poor Finn."

"He will survive." Mitzi giggled, but then,

remembering the gravity of the current situation, dropped her smile and turned to Dodge. "What do we do if help doesn't get here in time? Do we even stand a chance?"

Dodge turned his giant form to face Mitzi and looked her squarely in the eyes. "We absolutely do stand a chance. You'll see."

"I just don't want anyone to get hurt," Mitzi said. "Maybe I should just give myself up. I mean, they only want…"

"Girl, you are out of your mind if you think any of us will let that happen," Rose interrupted.

"She is right," Dodge said. "Enough of that. Linda will have an answer. I feel in my gut that help will be here soon."

"I hope your guts are right," Mitzi said, and the three stood watching as the very last of the light disappeared from the night sky.

Chapter Thirty-Five

About fifteen minutes passed before Linda drove up in the golf cart. Mitzi heard the cart well before she could see it and the wide-eyed Linda rolling up to the steps. "We have a problem!" she was shouting. "Where is Captain Frank? He has betrayed us all. He never made the call for help! He's with them!"

"Wait, what?" Mitzi yelled back. "He has Finn!"

Without a word, Mitzi and Rose ran from the steps at top speed toward the bathrooms, searching for their friend, followed closely by Dodge, shouting behind them, "Wait! You can't just run off! It could be a trap!"

But Mitzi didn't care if it was a trap. She had

to find Finn.

"Finn!" she yelled as they neared the bathrooms.

"Finnster!" Rose yelled.

"In here," Finn's muffled voice rang out from the boy's room.

Relief flooded through Mitzi as she ran into the bathroom and was instantly rattled to see Finn, crouched on the floor, with his hands tied to the sink pipes.

"That jerk tied me to the pipes with my own shoelaces," he yelled as he did his best to move out of the way so Mitzi could untie him.

"Are you alright, though?" Rose asked as Mitzi worked at untying the fiddley knots.

"I'm fine," Finn said, shaking his head. "But I can't believe Frank is helping those monsters."

"Did he say anything?" Mitzi said as she freed

the last knot. "Did he give you any clues as to what the heck he is doing helping them?"

"No," Finn said. "He just snapped and caught me off guard. He held up a knife and told me to sit on the floor and take off my shoes. I didn't know what the heck was going on so I just did what he told me to do. Then he took out the laces and tied my hands to the pipes."

"That's messed up," Rose said.

"He just mumbled, 'I'm sorry,' and then ran off," Finn said, rubbing his wrists as he stood. "What the heck is going on?"

"I think they finally got coms working in the tower," Mitzi said. "Turns out that Frank never made that call for help."

"Oh no!" Finn said. "Does that mean we are on our own then?"

"Only for a little while." Dodge's voice

startled the three of them as he stepped into the bathroom. "Help is a little over an hour away."

"Any word about Seph and the guys?" Rose asked.

"No," Dodge said softly.

A sudden and loud howl ripped through the night, followed by several more. Dodge's eyes grew as wide as lightbulbs and he pulled the door open in a swift motion. "We gotta get back now!" he shouted. "Run!"

The four ran back to the main cabin in a flash and found Linda, scanning the dark fields from the porch. "I think they are coming," she whispered. "Get inside now."

Dodge, Rose, and Finn climbed up the steps and went inside, but Mitzi took a deep breath as she stood next to Linda. "I think you should give me up," she said. "I will be okay. They want the blood vial.

They won't hurt me because I am their bargaining chip, and SHUT will think of a way to save me."

Linda looked at Mitzi, her forehead piled with wrinkles and her mouth in a sharp frown. "No, they won't. SHUT will never negotiate with them. That blood vial is worth way more than one girl. They would just kill you, Mitzi."

"But my dad would make sure…"

"Mitzi," Linda interrupted firmly. "You father is hours and hours away. He would never get here in time to do anything to help. We are on our own for now. So, do as I say and just get inside."

Mitzi's shoulders dropped and she slowly moved inside, closing the door behind her. She joined Rose and Finn, who were both standing at the window in a crowd of others, all trying to get a glimpse of what may be coming.

There was movement in the darkness.

"I know you are out there!" Linda yelled. "We will not give you what you want so you should just leave now."

A grumbly laughter returned from the fields. "If you won't give her to us, we will just come and take her," a deep gravelly voice blurted.

"No you won't," Linda said firmly. "You Vamps will never be invited in and we are heavily armed with silver. You would be foolish to even try. It's best if you just leave."

That was when Mitzi saw one of them. The blood in her whole body turned to ice as the full moon light shone on the forms in the field. They creatures were not wolf, yet clearly not human either. In the center of the field, stepping close to the outer salt ring, stood a very tall, very hairy werewolf form. He had pointed ears and a long snout full of sharp, dripping teeth and his broad and hairy ribcage heaved with each breath. Mitzi strained her eyes to see that its hands were curled with razor sharp claws. Two smaller wolves stood just behind him, equally as terrifying to look at.

Behind them, the four Vampires seemed to glide across the grounds, stopping just behind the human-esque canines. Although each of the Vamps were horrifying on their own, sharp fangs shining in the moonlight. It was the look on Alex's face that sent waves of panic through Mitzi. His face was contorted with rage and drool was sliding out of his mouth like a rapid dog.

Mitzi held her breath as the werewolf started to speak. It was unexpected. She didn't think they would speak in English. In the movies she had seen, the werewolves were always more dog than human, but now, in the field, she could see the opposite was true.

His voice was deep and airy. "If you don't let us in, we will just make you come out."

Thunk. The main cabin was thrown into darkness and screams of panic overwhelmed Mitzi's ears.

"Flashlights on!" Mr. Ross yelled. "Center of the room, shine your beams out, and I'll get the UV lights on."

The campers rushed in a chaotic panic to the center of the giant room, but Mitzi, Rose, and Finn didn't move from their spot at the window. Within moments, Mr. Ross had the generator on and the UV lights shone brightly onto the grass in front of the building and on the cluster of campers on the inside.

Mitzi turned to see the campers, most of which were shaking and crying, unable to cope with what was happening. Some of the older kids were clutching weapons and bravely trying to protect the smaller ones.

Mitzi's heart was racing and a fire churned inside her stomach. She had to protect them. She had to think of something. That was when she heard them. They started quietly at first, but soon became overwhelmingly loud.

Whispers.

Sharp and dark whispers. They were growing from the corners of the room. The shadowy corners came to life, growing darker by the second. Whispers on top of whispers…of a hundred dark voices, echoing into a mighty roar. Flashlight beams jumped from corner to corner, each camper trying to pinpoint the source of the cacophony, but Mitzi knew. She knew the Shadow Men were there. Mitzi held her hands over her ears, which were burning from the volume. Rose had her face buried into Finn's shoulder with her fingers in each ear. Finn stood with a flashlight in each hand, held high above his head, shining them down upon the trio.

Unable to fix her eyes onto any one form, Mitzi could feel their energies darting around her in the shadows.

And they were angry.

***

"What do we do now?" Rose shouted as she frantically swished her flashlight through the dark, a terrified look on her face. "They are getting braver!"

Several dark forms circled around the room, using every inch of shadow to taunt the frightened campers.

"I think we need to get out of here," Finn said as he pointed his beam toward the door.

"And do what exactly?" Mitzi said. "I know this is horrible but as long as we have the lights, they can't hurt us here."

But just as she spoke, an eruption of glass and a stream of light flew over their heads; a fire tipped arrow landed with a thwack on the far wall, igniting the wood in a flash. Several screams pierced the air as the flames grew, filling the place with black smoke.

Several faceless campers started yelling.

"They can move through the smoke!"

"We have to get out of here!"

"The place is on fire!"

"What do we do?"

"I don't want to die!"

Mitzi's mind raced. They needed to get out of the burning building, but then what?

"Out onto the porch, everyone," Mr. Ross shouted, coughing from the smoke. "Keep your weapons ready and don't get off the porch until you are told."

It was chaos. The doors overloaded with

frightened and panicked campers, each trying to make their way to safety while trying to keep the Shadow Men from getting close in the smoke. Mitzi watched in horror as Mimi was accidentally pushed and fell onto the floor, dropping her flashlight and swarmed by darkness as she kicked and screamed.

Mitzi swung her flashlight through the air like a sword, cutting the creatures away from her. Mimi sat up, covered in sweat, and vomited on the floor.

"Thank you," she choked out as she wiped her mouth with her elbow. Mitzi nodded and helped her off the floor, and could barely see through the smoke anymore.

"Let's stay low and get out," Mitzi said, dragging Mimi to the exit. There was barely an inch to stand on the porch, and with the fire blazing behind them, Mitzi knew they would have to come up with something else, and fast.

Suddenly, the UV lights clicked out, sending another audible gasp through the crowd.

"Get down here, kids, and stay close!" Linda shouted, and Mitzi could hear more dark laughter from the monsters.

"That was too easy," Alex yelled over the now roaring blaze. "We have you surrounded now."

"Surrounded?" Mitzi turned to the burning building behind them and her breath ran out of her at the sight of the flaming Shadow Men standing in a line on the porch.

There was at least a dozen of them. Black forms, engulfed in flames, standing shoulder to shoulder. Mitzi stared at them in horror as they burned without reaction, glowing with the occasional flash of a true skeletal form, showing through their dark black forms.

"Ahhhhh!" Dodge screamed a war cry, and

Mitzi turned in time to see him rush straight at the head werewolf, swinging his weapon, followed by the security guard and Mr. Ross, each with knives held high.

Dodge's spiked ball connected with the tall werewolf's head and he fell, but before he could even hit the ground, a Vampire swooped over and knocked Dodge to the ground and bit down on his neck. Mitzi tried to look away but couldn't. His legs shook and his body quickly went limp.

Mr. Ross didn't stand a chance and as he charged another werewolf, the werewolf crouched down and grabbed him by the waist, flinging him around and throwing him through the air. He screamed as he went several feet before landing with a hard thud. He lay unmoving, crumpled on the ground.

The security guard didn't have any more luck

than the other two as two Vampires swooped in and grabbed him under his armpits and slammed him on the ground. Just as they were about to strike his neck, the swoosh of an arrow whizzed overhead and struck one of the Vamps in the center of the back. He fell to the ground, screaming as his wound smoked and sizzled. Mitzi watched as burning embers spread out from his wounds, consuming him as he wriggled and screamed, until he was a pile of ash.

"Water guns!" Linda shouted. "Now."

Sprays of silver water erupted from everywhere, making contact with the werewolves, who howled in pain as their skin sliced and burned, sending them into retreat until they were out of range, the leader bleeding from the head, where Dodge connected his weapon.

Mitzi felt something cold hit her cheek, and then her forehead. Rain.

"That isn't good!" Finn yelled. "If it rains now, the fire will go out and that light is all that's keeping those Shadow Men from attacking!"

"Not to mention, the salt ring will be washed away," Rose added.

Thwack. Another arrow whizzed through the air and struck another Vampire in the chest. Mitzi looked all around and couldn't see where it was coming from but was extremely grateful for the archer. That left them with only Alex, and one other Vampire, four injured werewolves, and a dozen Shadow Men still to contend with, but at least they were getting somewhere.

If only help would get there.

A rush of wind took Mitzi's breath away and the next thing she knew, she was being held up in the air, inches from Alex's face. His breath was hot and smelled of rotting flesh. He pushed her head to the side to bare her neck and brought his fangs against her skin.

She didn't dare take a breath. Her body shook in fear but she was determined to not cry out. Rose and Finn ran out after her, but Linda grabbed their arms, holding them back.

"You can't do anything," she cried. "Please, Alex, don't hurt her! She's just a child."

The werewolves started back toward Alex, knowing that they had the upper hand now, laughing as they took their place by his side.

"Just a child," Alex snarled, and Mitzi could feel him tremble with emotion. "My beautiful Ivy was just a child! No one protected her!"

"Alex," Linda pleaded. "Don't do this. Hurting another child won't bring Ivy back. She would not want this."

"Don't you dare tell me what she would

want!" he snapped. "SHUT doesn't care about any of us."

"So you are just gonna hurt the innocent then?" Linda pushed. "To get even with SHUT?"

"That's right," he said. "If the creatures are in the open, then no one will ever go through what I've gone through, what I have lost." A single tear rolled down his face.

"But what about all the pain you are causing right now?" Mitzi whispered as she strained to look Alex in the eye. She wanted to get through to him and make him see what he was doing. The poem she had read, circled in his book, came to her and with a strained voice, she recited the only part she could remember. "If I could stop one heart from breaking, I should not live in vain."

Alex's grip relaxed and his face crumpled at the sound of his beloved Ivy's favorite poem. Mitzi pushed on. "Ivy was so beautiful and she was a hero, Alex. She would never want you to do this."

Mitzi could feel the air run out of Alex as he set her back down on the ground. "Mitzi," he said, starting to sob. "I'm so sorry. I…

Thwack. An arrow pierced him right in the forehead and he dropped backward onto the ground, motionless.

Mitzi stared as his body crumbled to the ground. Stunned by his quick end as she watched him start to smoke and burn.

"What are you doing, Mitzi?" Finn yelled. "Run!"

But it was too late.

A werewolf was running at her, full speed, growling and drooling, his eyes glowing red in the moonlight as he raced toward her. He leaped through the air, and Mitzi crossed her arms in front of her face to brace for the impact.

But a man came running in from out of nowhere and tackled the beast, intercepting her attacker and knocking him into the ground. Mitzi was confused in the darkness. It was Captain Frank fighting the beast with all his might. Clearly overpowered by the werewolf, who quickly pinned him to the ground and viscously chomped down on his neck as he cried out in pain.

Finn grabbed the stunned Mitzi by the hand, pulling her behind himself, and sprayed silver water at the beast, who snarled and cried out in pain before scrambling away and out of sight.

Mitzi ran to the bleeding form of Captain Frank on the ground. His breath was coming in short gasps as blood rushed from the gaping wound on his neck. The rain falling harder now, she kneeled beside him and held his face in her hand. She looked at the wound, deep and grizzly, knowing there was nothing that could be done.

"No one," Frank mumbled, "hurt. No one…hurt."

Mitzi brought her face close to his. She wanted to hear what he was trying to say. "No one was supposed to get hurt?" she asked.

"Right," he said, now gasping and choking on each breath. "Only trade…no death," he said.

"I understand, Frank," Mitzi said. "I will make sure they know you didn't want anyone to be hurt. But why did you do this? Why did you help them get in?"

"My darling Ivy," he said, coughing. "They were supposed to protect her. She was supposed to stay here…"

"Here at camp?" Mitzi asked.

"Yes, but they made her go," he wheezed.

"SHUT killed her, so I wanted to take them down."

Mitzi couldn't tell the difference between the rain on his cheeks and his tears, but knew the tears were there. Ivy was his daughter. That was how he came to work with Alex in this horrible plot.

"I am," he drew in a raspy deep breath, and said with his last breath, "so…sorry."

Mitzi wanted to tell him that she understood. Her heart broke for the man, but at the same time, knew that he had caused so much harm. She turned and scanned the area around her.

The fire was nearly out from the rains and the Shadow Men were coming down from the porch and approaching the fields, where staff and kids were frantically spraying silver water, sweeping their flashlight beams like swords, and shooting arrows in every direction. The rain was so heavy now that Mitzi could not make out where anyone was, other than

Finn, who still stood by her side, ready with his own weapon.

"Where is Rose?" she yelled over the rain. "I can't see anything!"

"I don't know," he yelled. "But the Shadow Men are attacking us now so keep your light handy and let's see if we can find her, or Linda."

He grabbed her hand and they ran around the battlefield, sweeping their beams from side to side as they looked for help.

"There!" Finn yelled, pointing to Linda, who was using her flashlight like a sword, slashing away a Shadow Man from three frightened girls.

"Linda!" Mitzi yelled. "Frank and Alex are Dead. We need to take shelter and regroup."

Linda turned and her crazed face was soaked, her eyes full with terror. She shouted loudly, "Retreat to the Pavilion. There are auxiliary lights in there!

Retreat to the pavilion."

Mitzi and Finn stood and watched as campers ran by, scanning for any signs of Rose. "She's not here!" Mitzi yelled.

"Maybe we just missed her, Mitzi!" he said, grabbing her arm and running after the crowd. "We gotta run. We're not safe here."

They ran and ran and the earth squished under their feet. Mitzi could just barely make out the sounds of the horrible whispers through the rain, chasing behind them. Ahead, she could see the lights come on in the pavilion and a surge of hope rushed through her, knowing they were almost there.

A sudden fire stabbed through her leg, dropping her face first into the mud. She lost Finn's grip and was being dragged back into the darkness. She fought to flip over to see what was dragging her, terrified by the sight of a werewolf. His canine snout clamped down on her leg, dragging her like a piece of meat. She kicked with her free foot as hard as she could but it was no use. His strength far exceeding her own, he was barely bothered by her protestation.

"Let go of me," Mitzi cried out in pain and felt a hand reach for hers. She looked to see Finn, fighting to pull her back.

"You can't take her," he yelled as he pulled.

Mitzi's leg burned with the pain of a million glass shards stabbing at her as he pulled. Her shoulder and hand searing in pain as Finn fought to maintain his grip in the slippery rain. She could feel his hold loosening.

"Finn!" she cried. "Please hold on."

"I am trying," he groaned. "I… can't… hold… on."

Mitzi broke free from Finn's grip and slid several feet through the mud. She let out a scream and *thwack*, she was suddenly free from the beast, who was yelping and howling, spinning on the ground in pain, clawing at the arrow jutting out from its neck, until, at last, it fell, dead.

"Come on," Finn said, lifting Mitzi off the ground, scooping her up in his arms. "We've got to get you help."

Mitzi buried her head in Finn's cold, wet shoulder. Her leg was throbbing with fire and she could feel her strength running out. Finn was mumbling but she could not make out the words. She couldn't lift up her head. She was falling into darkness. Everything slipped away.

Chapter Thirty-Six

"Mitzi," a sweet voice sounded far away in the darkness.

"Sweetheart," it said as it grew closer, "please wake up now."

Mitzi cracked open her eyes to see Ms. Stukes standing over her, rubbing her forehead and smiling. In a rush, reality stormed through Mitzi and she tried to sit up, but was quickly pushed back down.

"You are safe now, child," Ms. Stukes said softly. "We are all safe. SHUT is here now."

"Finn…" Mitzi groaned, and was hit with a sharp pain in her leg. "Rose?"

"They have only *just* left your side," she said, smiling. "Minutes ago. I made them go get something to eat. The sun has been up for hours."

"Are the monsters gone?" Mitzi asked. "Did we win? Will I be a werewolf now?"

Ms. Stukes's face fell. "The Vampires and werewolves are dead. The Shadow Men cannot be killed but have no power in the day, so are not a threat for now." She bit the inside of her cheek and rubbed Mitzi's forehead again. "As far as your other question…I don't think anyone won anything. We lost three of our teachers, two of our security guards, and one student. Several others were bitten but, like yourself, were given the antidotes in time to avoid transformation."

"What about Seph? And Jeremy? Malakai?" Mitzi asked as her heart pounded. "Did they make it back?"

"Make it back?" Ms. Stukes laughed. "Not only did they make it back, but, darling, they saved the day! Seph was the one that took out that beast that was chomping on your leg. A lot of heroes emerged last night, that's for sure."

"Seph was the archer that saved my life?" Mitzi said, tears building up in her eyes.

Seph's voice came from behind her. "That's right, freckles. I couldn't stand by and watch you become dog food, now, could I?"

"Thank you," Mitzi said. "Was that you the whole night with the arrows?"

"Nope," she said. "Just that last one. Millie was the amazing sniper of the evening. At first, she was shooting from the tower, then she moved to the staff house roof, and then she even climbed a tree. She's like a pint-sized assassin! Made four kills in all. Not bad for a cover kid who didn't even know about SHUT until a few days ago."

"I'd say," Mitzi said. "Is she okay?"

"She will live," Seph said, smiling warmly at

Mitzi.

"What were you thinking?" Mitzi asked. "With the boat and all. Are the guys alright? Did you make contact?"

"We got out a couple hours and the seas were nasty," she said. "We had to turn back before we got close enough to call for help. We hid in the marina thinking maybe we could launch a surprise attack. But then we saw the pavilion lights come on and ran to help. Just in time, too."

"Ugh," Mitzi said. "I've never been a chew toy before."

"So you've got jokes now, huh?" Rose said as her and Finn approached.

"Rose!" Mitzi said, feeling emotion rise in her throat. "I was so worried. I'm so glad you're alright."

"Girl, I'm fine," she said, tears forming at the corner of her tired eyes. "You scared the crap out of us, though."

"Crazy, though, right?" Finn said. "Alex's lost love was Captain Frank's Daughter. Who would have seen that coming?"

"How could Linda have not known that connection?" Mitzi said suspiciously.

"I'll take that one," Ms. Stukes chimed in. "You see, when Ivy died, there was no formal funeral. We don't have funerals for most SHUT agents, and the member registry only lists her father as John Frank. Ivy's last name was Moore. Her parents were divorced when she was a child and she took her mother's name. Her mother was not a member of SHUT so because she had full custody of Ivy, she was listed as a cover kid. No one knew that Captain Frank was her dad. No one here at camp, anyway. He never told us. Never told anyone."

"But how would Linda not know that Captain

Frank's first name was John?" Mitzi was practically shouting.

"I really believe it was an oversight," Ms. Stukes said softly. "We have all known Captain Frank for well over a decade. It never even occurred to me that his first name wasn't Frank. You just kind of forget that Frank is a last name, I guess."

"A deadly oversight," Mitzi sadly said, shaking her head when another thought occurred to her. "You said a student died? Who was it?"

Mitzi looked at Finn and Rose, who both looked down at the ground, avoiding her question. Her eyes met with Seph's and locked.

"It was Bella," Seph said as Mitzi felt a rock twist inside her chest. "A Vamp was about to get Mimi and Jayde. She tried to stake it through the chest, but he was too fast. Bit her right in front of them and drained her completely. So horrible."

"Millie finished the job for her before he could get the twins, though," Rose said. "Shot him right in the chest."

"Thank God for Millie," Mitzi said as the others nodded their agreement. "So, what now? Does anyone know? I mean, we obviously aren't staying at camp."

"They're arranging flights home for all of us now," Seph said. "It's the cover kids that are a bit trickier. SHUT families may end up hosting them for a few days before they figure that mess out. But we will all be out of here before night falls."

"Rose and Finn," Mitzi said, smiling at her two best friends, "I guess you will be coming home with me."

"Sounds good to me," Finn said.

Rose grabbed Mitzi's hand and gave it a squeeze. "Same."

Epilogue

"Okay, guys, keep it down," Mitzi's father Ben said from his spot on the couch as he increased the volume on the living room television.

Rose, Mitzi, and Finn were playing cards on the floor, laughing about some stupid joke that Finn had made.

"Sorry, Dad," Mitzi said, absent mindedly scratching her healing leg. It was always itching like crazy, even after several weeks of healing, a side effect from the medication which was a small price to pay to avoid becoming a werewolf.

"In other news," the TV reporter's voice blared throughout the room, "there have been several odd reports coming out of New Orleans. Apparently, several people have reported seeing dog-like creatures, standing on two legs and running through the streets. These sightings have occurred in several neighborhoods and, interestingly enough, only during the full moon."

The living room was eerily quiet as everyone turned their attention to the television.

"Authorities urge the community not to be alarmed and believe this to be a well-planned and elaborate hoax."

"On the lighter side of things, the Centerville Pet Adoption Fair is coming into town…" the reporter said cheerfully as Ben clicked off the TV, set the remote down, and rubbed his face.

"This can't be good," Mitzi said, shaking her head. "What are we gonna do now, Dad?"

"This seems like it may be the beginning of some dark times ahead," he said. "They are growing bolder by the day and war is imminent, I'm afraid."

Mitzi looked at Finn and Rose. Their expressions matched the dread that Mitzi was feeling inside.

"They won't stop until they get their hands on the last vial," he said. "Obviously, we can't let that happen."

"We need to get the Vampire vial and the werewolf vials back," Finn said. "But how the heck do we do that? Do we know where they are keeping them?"

"We're working on it," he said. "We are working on bio trackers that can scan large areas for shapes specific to werewolves. Also, scanning systems that specifically seek out movements without a heat signature."

"Too bad camp didn't have that technology," Rose said. "Is that the special project that Trent is working on with his father?"

"Sure is," Ben said. "He's such a smart kid. Can't believe he was the one to get the coms working at camp. God only knows what would have happened without him."

"He's coming over later for dinner," Mitzi said, her face flushing.

"So glad he's not the jerk he was at camp." Rose laughed. "Those Shadow Men are no joke."

"Truth," Finn agreed. "I haven't slept without the light on since we've been back."

"That's understandable," Ben said. "They are nasty creatures for sure."

"I still can't believe that SHUT is swearing in so many underage kids as full-fledged members this weekend," Mitzi said. "But I guess we need all the help we can get so it makes sense."

"Who all exactly is taking their pledge?" Finn asked.

"Seph, Jeremy, and Malakai," Ben said. "They are the new Team Shark, for their bravery on the ocean and their attempts to save camp."

"Plus, Seph saved my life," Mitzi added.

"Millie," Ben said. "We all know how her actions saved several lives."

Mitzi smiled. "She was amazing," she said. "Plus Trent, for his miracle with the communications, and that senior that saved Linda from a Vamp ... what was his name?"

"Logan Jones," Ben said. "Together, those three will be Team Scorpion. They have all more than proven their worth in the organization and we are lucky to have each one of them."

"I'm worried about what's gonna happen, Dad," Mitzi said. "I feel like this whole thing is like a bomb about to blow. Can we really stop them?"

"That's a fair concern, Mitzi," Ben said. "The

Dark Trinity cannot be released. We have so much to do in order for us to be able to stop them. If their existence becomes public, if they go into the open, the whole world will panic."

"Why not destroy the one vial we have?" Finn asked. "Then there would be no chance of the Dark Trinity returning."

"It's complicated, Finn," he said. "But hopefully we will reclaim the first two vials and all three can be destroyed in the near future."

Mitzi looked at her father and a realization struck her. She and her friends were the new generation of SHUT fighters. It would be up to them to stop the war from becoming a reality. It was time to come up with a plan.

Now was the time to recover the missing vials and destroy them, once and for all.

www.ingramcontent.com/pod-product-compliance
Lightning Source LLC
LaVergne TN
LVHW041655060526
838201LV00043B/443